**"It'd be bette[...]
upright. Can y[...]**

"Piece of cake," Carson said, bracing one arm on the exam table. "Have at it."

But somewhere under all that pain he was grateful for the chance to be near Bridget, to hear her soothing tone and see the care in her eyes.

"See if you can manage to bleed less," she joked.

"Yes, ma'am," he said.

Bridget leaned closer and assessed the wound. Even over the sharp scent of the antiseptic, he could smell her shampoo or lotion or perfume. It was enough to make him dizzy even without the wallop to his head.

She touched his forehead, a sensation as soothing to him as any bunny bandages were to the youngsters. "A few butterfly bandages should do the trick. Unless you'd like a tough-guy scar—stitches do a better job of that."

"No thanks. I like my face the way it is."

"Me, too," she said softly, then cleared her throat. "I'm all for scar prevention."

But she hadn't quite covered the slip…and they both knew it.

Allie Pleiter, an award-winning author and RITA® Award finalist, writes both fiction and nonfiction. Her passion for knitting shows up in many of her books and all over her life. Entirely too fond of French macarons and lemon meringue pie, Allie spends her days writing books and avoiding housework. Allie grew up in Connecticut, holds a BS in speech from Northwestern University and lives near Chicago, Illinois.

Books by Allie Pleiter

Love Inspired

True North Springs

A Place to Heal
Restoring Their Family
The Nurse's Homecoming

Wander Canyon

Their Wander Canyon Wish
Winning Back Her Heart
His Christmas Wish
A Mother's Strength
Secrets of Their Past

Matrimony Valley

His Surprise Son
Snowbound with the Best Man
Wander Canyon Courtship

Visit the Author Profile page at LoveInspired.com for more titles.

The Nurse's Homecoming

Allie Pleiter

LOVE INSPIRED
INSPIRATIONAL ROMANCE

If you purchased this book without a cover you should be aware that this book is stolen property. It was reported as "unsold and destroyed" to the publisher, and neither the author nor the publisher has received any payment for this "stripped book."

LOVE INSPIRED®
INSPIRATIONAL ROMANCE

Recycling programs for this product may not exist in your area.

ISBN-13: 978-1-335-58658-2

The Nurse's Homecoming

Copyright © 2023 by Alyse Stanko Pleiter

All rights reserved. No part of this book may be used or reproduced in any manner whatsoever without written permission except in the case of brief quotations embodied in critical articles and reviews.

This is a work of fiction. Names, characters, places and incidents are either the product of the author's imagination or are used fictitiously. Any resemblance to actual persons, living or dead, businesses, companies, events or locales is entirely coincidental.

For questions and comments about the quality of this book, please contact us at CustomerService@Harlequin.com.

Love Inspired
22 Adelaide St. West, 41st Floor
Toronto, Ontario M5H 4E3, Canada
www.LoveInspired.com

Printed in U.S.A.

All the paths of the Lord are mercy and truth unto
such as keep his covenant and his testimonies.
—*Psalm* 25:10

To all who generously give the gift of life
by donating organs or bone marrow

Chapter One

Bridget Nicholson parked her car in the gravel parking lot of Camp True North Springs and hoped her shock wasn't visible through the windshield.

It couldn't be.

It was.

As she stared at the camp staff assembled to greet her, she was met with the sight of the one man who could make this job a bigger challenge than it already was: Carson Todd.

Up until this moment, Bridget had thought her father's disapproval of this job had been her biggest hurdle. He'd wanted her to have nothing to do with Camp True North Springs. It was "beneath her potential," he'd said. As if she could—and should—do much better than becoming a camp's temporary nurse to "those problem families."

The Camp True North Springs families were indeed a far cry from the posh vacationers she'd tended to on the cruise ship *Brilliance*. Still, Bridget couldn't see how families who had lost a member to violence deserved Dad's unfair disdain. Everyone deserved care.

What was also unfair—decidedly—was how good Carson looked. Her attempts to drag her gaze away and focus on her two employers failed. The past three years had changed him. His sandy-brown hair—unkempt and wild in the past—was cut close and clean. His intense blue eyes bore a more settled look. His lean, tanned body had filled out to a stronger and sturdier build. The younger man who'd loped around without much focus now stood with a capable, grounded stance. Everything and nothing like the Carson Todd Dad had insisted she leave behind.

To say she and Carson had history together was an understatement larger than the mountain behind her. How could she spend the next four weeks in close quarters with this man? One who had once been the love of her life? Her confidence trickled away.

Don't you back down now, she told herself as

she got out of her car. *You've been around the world—twice—on a luxury cruise liner, you can handle four weeks on an Arizona mountainside.* Bridget stood as tall as her five-foot-four frame would allow and extended a hand to the couple walking toward her. She forced confidence into her voice.

"Hello, Mason. Hello, Dana." She stopped there, not knowing any of the other staff and certainly not ready to say "Hello, Carson," even though her gaze kept rebelliously slipping toward the man. Evidently, Carson was having the same problem, for he was doing a poor job of trying to appear casual while looking everywhere but at her.

"Hello, Bridget," Mason Avery replied, offering a friendly handshake. "Welcome to Camp True North Springs." His cordial tone faltered as he bounced his glances between Bridget and Carson. So... Mason *knew* this was an awkward reunion. His wife, Dana, seemed to know, as well. Did they all know? Bridget's insides recoiled at the thought of everyone knowing her romantic history with Carson. A breakup so dramatic that it had sent her halfway around the world.

Up until a month ago, travel had been a wonderful thing. She'd given in to her father's request—his demand, actually, that she leave Carson behind—and had turned Dad's sizable travel allowance into the adventure of a lifetime. That adventure had brought her to Anders. They had been building a life together.

Had been building. As in *no longer*.

As in my left hand no longer has a diamond ring on it. Adding Carson's presence to the wounds of her broken engagement seemed to add insult to injury.

Had Dad known? Had he purposefully hidden Carson's presence at the camp from her? It would be something he would do.

Bringing her thoughts back to the present moment, Bridget shook off the flurry of emotions and hid behind a professional demeanor. "I'm glad to be here." *Don't look at Carson.* Instead, Bridget turned her attention to the boy standing between Dana and Mason. He looked about nine, and she remembered reading something about him just finishing third grade. Too bad it was mid-June and school wasn't in session. School nurse sounded far safer than her current predicament.

"You must be Charlie." She kept her voice bright. "What's it like to run a camp at your age?"

Charlie's laugh broke some of the tension,

smiling up at his father and stepmother. "I don't run it. Dad and Dana do. And everyone else. The new friends start getting here tomorrow."

New friends. Five families would be arriving on-site tomorrow, each recovering from a personal tragedy. She knew a bit about the Garza family—they had been the ones to recommend her for this job—but the rest would be new acquaintances.

"We were so glad Martina suggested you," Dana said as they walked toward the group of other staff—including Carson, who took a step back and looked down at his boots as she approached. "You're an answer to our prayer. Everyone will feel so much better with a nurse on-site while little Matteo is here."

Bridget nodded. "It works out for everyone. I can fill in while figuring out my next steps, and Martina can relax knowing we're ready for whatever Matteo might need."

"He looks like such a sweet little guy," Dana said. "You must know him if you know Martina."

"Actually, Martina and I hadn't kept in touch until recently. I admit the referral took me a bit by surprise, but it worked out great for everyone, didn't it?" Bridget had grown up with

Martina in North Springs and had only kept in casual touch over social media. Martina knew Bridget had broken off her engagement to Anders and was coming back home after finishing her contract with the cruise line. Bridget knew Martina's husband had been killed in a military accident earlier this year and that her son had medical challenges.

"We hadn't planned to add an on-site nurse until later in the season," Mason said. "But no one wanted to say no to those two after all they've been through."

Bridget couldn't imagine saying no to any of the families she knew were soon to arrive. Each one was battling grief and needing space to heal. Her heart had broken as she'd skimmed through the family profiles Dana had sent over earlier. Her own troubles seemed trivial by comparison.

"It was an easy yes for me," Bridget agreed. "Martina seems to need what you're offering here. All the families do."

Dana nodded. "I couldn't agree more."

"I wish your father felt that way, if you don't mind my saying," Mason replied. "I almost didn't ask and was surprised you said yes."

Bridget offered her new employer a knowing look. "I'm not my dad."

Carson was standing just close enough for Bridget to hear the small grunt he gave at that statement. They'd have to talk about their past breakup at some point, but not here and not now.

Dad's negative view of Camp True North Springs stumped her. Who could be against providing healing and respite to grieving families? Dad's position that the camp brought "problem families" to the town was just plain wrong. Yes, poverty and lack of opportunity led some people toward violence, but Bridget could tell surprisingly painful stories from her upscale patients aboard the *Brilliance*, too. In her experience, pain and loss ignored the size of anyone's bank account.

Bridget tried again to keep her gaze off Carson, despite an avalanche of questions. What had he done in the years since they'd been together? It made sense he was still in North Springs—he'd never quite found his path after high school. No college, no big plans, just a laidback, in-the-moment guy. Dad had found that intolerable, but his sense of easy freedom had appealed to Bridget. Carson paid close attention to his life. He was too engrossed in today to worry much about tomorrow. Life for him was plain and satisfying. When something went wrong, he simply fixed it and moved forward.

Bridget couldn't consider that an accomplished life. His attitude would never lead to the bright future her family valued so highly. Then again, had all *her* planning achieved a bright future? Did Carson know about her engagement? Or the fact that she'd broken it off?

"Hello, Bridget." Carson chose that moment to break the silence between them. "I'm the fix-it guy around here. Nice to see you again." The timbre of his deep, rich voice struck her anew. It had been one of the things that had first drawn her to him.

Mason shifted his weight. "Carson told me you two…know each other. I had no idea, or I might have said something." After a fidgety pause, Mason added, "I want my staff to feel comfortable. Is this going to be a problem?"

"No," Bridget and Carson declared loudly at the same time.

"It'll be fine," Bridget added.

"All good," Carson chimed in.

Bridget had doubts that it would be fine or good, but she would make it work. They both would. While she would drive back down the mountain tonight and pack the last of her things, nothing—not even this gigantic new wrinkle—would stop her from coming back up to start her job tomorrow.

* * *

Carson spent an hour pretending to get work done. Pretending, because his mind refused to focus on any topic but Bridget. Finally, he gave up and went looking for her in the camp infirmary that had been set up in the back of the big house's main floor.

He found it empty but everything in tidy order. That was Bridget—organized to the hilt. There was a time when his own impulsive and disorganized nature—bad then, but a bit better now—drove her to distraction. Who was being driven to distraction now?

Hearing a noise from the room just down the hall, Carson walked over to find Bridget unloading a suitcase into the chest of drawers. She hadn't changed her hair much—the brown locks still framed her face in a clean, short cut. He'd always found her cute—small and tanned with luxurious brown eyes and a smile that could make him feel like king of the world. Still, she had a sophistication about her that caught him up short. As if she'd moved on— or up—in the world while he hadn't. He wondered, if they'd met today for the first time, if he'd find the confidence to pursue her the way he had all those years ago when he'd fallen hard for her.

Now, they'd be living within yards of each other. For a whole month. That proximity loomed between them like a giant minefield of romantic history.

He leaned against the open doorway and waited until she noticed him before asking, "Getting settled in?" He tried to sound casual, but her expression told him he'd failed. They had to get a handle on this awkwardness, and fast. He'd be thirty years old next year, she, twenty-eight—mature enough to find a way to make the next few weeks work.

"Starting to, at least." Her voice was tight and tense.

"That's good." He noticed the clothing in neat stacks behind her. Fancy, elegant things. Things belonging to a woman who had traveled the world. He'd heard of her job on the cruise ship, heard of her engagement to some important ship's officer. Carson had figured he wouldn't ever see her again.

She clasped her hands in front of her and shrugged, a gesture he remembered vividly. "I've got more things to bring up from the house tomorrow, but I'm almost done. Short stay, after all."

The room felt too close, too small to hold all

the history between them. "Want to walk out to the pond? I'm thinking maybe we should talk."

She hesitated at first, but eventually nodded and grabbed her ID lanyard and keys. As they left the big house, Carson pointed in the direction of the pond on the west side of the property. It was hot—June had already served up some scorcher days—but outside felt safer, and the pond was a good place for a private conversation.

"What's with him?" Bridget asked as they walked past a comical tin frog fountain spouting water under one of the trees off the house's front porch.

"Oh, that's Franco. It's a long story, but he was a stand-in of sorts for the big pond."

Bridget's dark brows furrowed over her expressive eyes. He could stare forever at those fascinating eyes back when they were together. At the moment, those eyes were filled with the same caution and confusion that had churned in his stomach since her arrival.

"Stand-in?" she asked. "For a pond?"

"There's a thing they do for the families," Carson explained. "Everyone sends a flower floating out across the pond for the person they've lost. Dana bought Franco for Charlie to do that for his mother back when the big pond was dried up." He gazed at the big round eyes of the frog, forever spouting water into his little ceramic pond. "Ask Charlie. He explains it best."

"He seems like an amazing kid," Bridget replied. "Especially when you think about what he's been through." She was quiet for a minute as they made their way down the path to the pond, but then continued, "I missed kids on the ship. There were a few now and then, but it was mostly older people." Her eyes shot Carson a look that resembled just a hint of the Bridget he remembered. "Rich, older people."

"Swanky boat, huh?"

His choice of words made her laugh. "Oh, don't you ever call the *Brilliance* a 'boat.' But yes, you could call it swanky." She gave her voice a dramatic travel-brochure tone and waved her hand in the air. "Luxurious staterooms, spectacular ports of call, top-notch cuisine, everything the discriminating traveler desires." She returned her voice to its normal friendliness. "Not exactly kid-friendly."

Carson tried to picture the down-to-earth, very kid-friendly Bridget he'd known on a ship like that. It didn't fit. But the woman in front of him at the moment? He could easily picture it. She was in a different league now—one far above his, that was for sure. "Did you like it? Working on board? Living on board?"

She shrugged again. "Who wouldn't like living how the 'other half' lives?"

"Swanky's never really been my thing. I can't picture myself doing what you did." The back of Carson's mind snagged on the unrelated fact that what she had done was leave him brokenhearted when her father had declared him "not good enough" to share a future with his daughter. If every conversation between them pointed back to their history, it would make for an excruciating month. Carson hadn't expected the old feelings of rejection to rise up so fresh and raw.

"Oh, it was always clear who was the passenger and who was the employee, but it was amazing. I saw so much of the world. Breathtaking sights. Met really interesting people."

And almost married one of them, Carson thought. No way was he going to bring that up. He'd let her decide when to talk about the ring now gone from her finger.

They'd finally reached the pond and Carson sat down on one end of the beautiful wooden bench by the small dock. Mason, who was a gifted carpenter, had built all the benches that graced the property. "I think the people *here* are really interesting. Not fancy—certainly not by your standards. But—" he searched for the right word, settling reluctantly on "—important. It's important what we do here. I'm glad to be a part of it." Would she get that? Value it the way he did? Or was she just here to mark time until her next important adventure?

Bridget sat down on the other end, keeping a healthy distance. "I know how Dad feels about this place."

Oh, so we are *going there*, Carson thought. *Okay, then.* "Everyone knows how your dad feels about this place. But he's wrong."

He waited for Bridget to agree with or refute his statement. When she didn't, he decided to ask, "Why *are* you here?"

She kept her silence for a while longer before replying. "The short answer is that Martina suggested it."

He still knew the look in her eyes well enough to say, "I can't think that's the only reason."

She softened. "I needed a place to think. Someplace the farthest thing from the *Brilliance* as I could find."

Carson settled back into the bench to kick his feet out in front of him. "So, swanky international grown-up ocean boat—*ship*," he corrected himself, "for perfect people versus cobbled-together desert family camp for wounded people. I think you nailed 'farthest thing.'"

She laughed. The slightly tight sound of it told him she hadn't done much laughing lately. Did she realize she kept running her fingers over the ring finger on her left hand? As if she needed to hide the bareness of it? *I can still see how you think*, he thought to himself. She wasn't okay. Far from it. The guy—swanky or not—had hurt her deeply.

After a stretch of silence, Carson dared to ask, "Are you okay?"

She answered his question with a direct, challenging glare.

"After everything," he continued, suddenly doubtful he should have asked. "Had to be hard. Big breakup like that. I heard."

"I'm *fine*." Her eyes warned against him suggesting otherwise.

No, she wasn't, and it stung a bit that she wouldn't admit that. To him, of all people. "It'd be fine if you weren't," he assured. "This is probably the one place in North Springs where *no one* pretends to be fine."

She narrowed her eyes at his use of the word "pretends"—and likely at his crack at the hypocrisy he found so hard to swallow in that town down the mountain. From Bridget's dad most of all. When they were dating, Bridget's dad had offered him a job at his insurance firm and hinted broadly that any "man of quality" ought to go to college. Carson's decline of both had been the beginning of Arthur's relentless campaign to end things between him and Bridget. And Arthur had won.

"Look, let's get one thing straight right now. I'm not thrilled you're here." Bridget sat up and squared off at him. "And I'm not thrilled Dad chose to keep that from me when he clearly knew."

"Me, neither," he replied. It was a classic Arthur Nicholson move. As to how he felt about Bridget's presence, Carson hadn't sorted that out yet.

"But I'm going to make the best of it," she continued. "I'm certainly not going to back down no matter how…awkward this is. It's not as if we'll be working closely together."

No, Carson thought, *it's just that we'll be living within yards of each other and eating together and serving the camper families and everything else.* "Not unless I bash my finger or something."

She didn't appreciate the joke. "I need to

know you see this as nothing more than an uncomfortable work situation. Don't go reading anything into it. It's not providence or reconciliation or anything like that."

Carson wasn't sure he liked the conclusions she was jumping to or the wall she was throwing up between them. "Could we be friends?" he ventured. She looked like someone who could use a friend.

Bridget glared at him. "To tell the truth, I'm not sure that's possible."

Chapter Two

"Why didn't you tell me?" Bridget blurted out as she burst into the family kitchen that evening. "You knew about Carson. You *had to* have known. Why didn't you tell me?"

Mom looked a bit sheepish, but Dad gave her a dismissive look. "I assumed Avery told you who else was on staff up there. And besides, I didn't think it would matter to you. You've obviously moved on, and that little thing was a long time ago."

That little thing. It irked Bridget that her father could dismiss the deep love she'd once had with Carson as *that little thing*. Then again, how else would he view the relationship he'd so effectively put a stop to? He'd never viewed Carson as anything but a minor poor choice on her part. Now the shoe was on the other foot;

Anders's parents had made their disapproval of her clear enough to doom her engagement. It gave her a new view of the pain Carson had likely known. And, if she were honest, a new sense of bitterness toward her father.

Bridget set down the empty boxes she planned to refill with her final things for tomorrow. Dad's condemnation of Carson was a topic for another day, but his deliberate omission needed to be dealt with now. "You should have said something. I didn't need to walk into that meeting to face a surprise like that. Everybody was uncomfortable. That's no way to start a job."

Dad looked surprised at the force of her words. She had more confidence now, but he wasn't taking kindly to the transformation. "That isn't a job," he grumbled. "They had to have known. And if they didn't, it only means Carson didn't see any reason to tell them." He raised a dubious eyebrow. "That says everything, doesn't it?"

"Don't blame this on Carson. He would have said something. He didn't know I was the new temporary nurse. Dana and Mason didn't know our…history." Determined to say her piece, she gave Dad a straight look and continued, "The only person who saw this coming was you, and you let me walk into it blind. Why?"

Mom glanced up from her cooking. "Don't speak to your father like that."

Bridget knew she could have shown more respect, but she'd had her fill of being found lacking and Mom's scolding tone only pricked another nerve.

"Did you think this would make me turn down the post?" After all, that would have worked on the old Bridget.

Dad returned to slicing the bread for dinner with an infuriating calm. "Well, I did hope this would make you consider going straight to a more respectable position elsewhere. You went to nursing school. You launched a career and a life with Anders. Why would you throw that away?"

Throw that away? Bridget didn't care much for more of the disappointment she had known under this roof. She picked the boxes back up and headed for the stairs. "I need to go finish packing."

"You're still going through with this?" Dad made it sound like the worst possible choice, as if it reinforced his poor opinion.

She turned on the bottom stair. "Why would I let *a little thing* like that stop me?" Awkward as it was up there on the mountain with Carson, it was a better place to sort things out than here.

It took a great amount of effort not to stomp up the stairs and refrain from slamming the door of her old bedroom like a teenager. The beautifully appointed room now felt stuffy and confining. Out the window, the mountain's silhouette sharpened against the sunset. The camp's space and clarity called to her. Deeply. She dumped the boxes at the foot of her bed and slumped into the bentwood rocking chair sitting under the window. It had always been her favorite place to think.

Carson. She'd been proud of how she had tucked him far back into her memory on the *Brilliance.* Convinced her father was right, she'd filed it away as just a dramatic phase of her former life. A young and impractical love. Not the mature, sophisticated relationship she'd had with Anders, the one with impressive careers and bright futures.

Or so she'd thought. She'd told herself she was imagining the first hints of Anders's family's ambivalence to their engagement. She'd tried to ignore their lukewarm welcome when he'd proposed. Anders's parents were exceedingly polite in their congratulations, but their best wishes lacked the heartfelt joy she'd expected. Anders had dismissed her reaction as just a cultural difference, but Bridget's worry had turned to dismay as their initial coldness persisted—and kept growing.

Soon it became impossible to ignore the Hagen family's disapproval of the match. She could see them wearing Anders down, filling him with doubts. In the end, she had called it off because it seemed easier to bear that than waiting for him to do it. She'd returned the enormous diamond engagement ring, arranged to finish out her contract on another ship and then limped home in defeat. At the moment, that seemed like an enormous mistake.

The sun had gone down behind the mountain when Mom's soft voice followed a knock on her door. "Bridget?"

"Come in, Mom."

Mom entered with a plate. "You sure you're not hungry?"

Bridget could only smile. "Actually, I am. Thanks."

After setting the plate on the bureau, Mom sat on the edge of the bed and smoothed out the bedspread beside her. "Are you really sure you still want to do this?"

Bridget didn't have the heart to say, "Especially now," but it was clear living here would only have her butting heads with Dad. They needed time and space. *She* needed time and space. "Yes," she answered her mother. "I can handle it. Carson and I are both adults, and it's only for a few weeks."

"But living up there?" Mom had asked more than once why she couldn't be the camp nurse during the day and come home at night. Mom wanted her little girl back under her roof, but Bridget couldn't find a way to tell her mother she wasn't that little girl anymore.

"I accepted this position. That includes living on-site. You didn't raise a daughter who would go back on her word just because things got a bit sticky." *A bit sticky* was an understatement. "You know how badly things ended with Carson. Maybe this will give us a way to part as coworkers. Friends, even," she offered, though she wasn't sure she believed that.

They sat for a few minutes in uncomfortable silence until Bridget worked up the nerve to ask, "Did you know Carson was there?" Bridget would have liked to think her mother would have told her, even if Dad had chosen to omit it.

She wasn't surprised when Mom replied, "No. I don't have anything to do with that camp. For obvious reasons. Some of the people around town began volunteering up there when things were first getting started, but they know better than to talk to us about it. Your father hasn't changed his mind about the place." Mom frowned. "You have to know how much it annoyed him that you chose to work there. You aren't good friends with Martina Garza. You barely knew each other. You don't owe her anything—certainly not this."

Some part of Bridget knew *exactly* how much it would annoy her father to be the camp nurse at Camp True North Springs. She'd told herself it was for a bunch of other reasons, including doing something nice for a little boy and an old schoolmate. However, if she was honest, it was also an act of rebellion.

Still, she listed all the nobler reasons she'd used to justify her choice. "It's just a few weeks. It'll give me time to work out what I do next and help Martina and her son at the same time. And if Dad's right, and it really is a bad thing, I'll know for sure."

Bridget rose and retrieved the dinner plate, ready to admit to her hunger over missing dinner. "I talked to the cook, Seb Costa, today. He told me about the first trial sets of families they'd had last summer. Mom, the stories were amazing. I think it will feel good to be part of something that important after just making fancy vacations for people."

Mom shrugged. "Fancy vacations are nice things."

Bridget let that comment sit while she ate a few bites of Mom's amazing cooking. The ship's elegant gourmet buffets were lovely, but there was something deeply comforting about Mom's roasted chicken and mashed potatoes.

"What is Carson doing up there, anyway?" Mom surprised her by asking. "I heard he went away for a while. Just aimless wandering. Living out of a van, someone said. But he came back."

Bridget didn't know about Carson living out of a van, but she did know how her father would view Carson's current job title. "He's the maintenance man."

"Oh." Her mother didn't quite hide her low assessment. Carson was clearly still a less-than-admirable man in her view.

"I could probably come home for dinner once a week," Bridget suggested. And just to see what the response would be, she added, "You know, you and Dad could always come up and visit me at the camp."

Mom's lips thinned. Both of them knew the likelihood of that ever happening.

* * *

Carson kicked dust off his boots as he watched Bridget lug the last boxes from her car into the big house. Part of him longed to go over and offer to help her carry in her belongings, but he told himself to keep his distance. In fact, *keep a wise distance* might need to be the thing he told himself constantly for the next few weeks. *You've got nothing to prove to her. Or anyone.*

It would be easier if Bridget's arrival didn't put such a twist in his gut. Yesterday had been shocking, then awkward, and then downright rough. Her presence brought a bunch of unexpected raw spots to the surface. *What are You up to, Lord? What possible good could come from her being here?*

His decision to skip the college path had been his choice. Working with his hands had always called to him. He craved the freedom of open spaces. He'd finally gotten to a place where he didn't feel the need to defend that. He felt good about himself and his place in the world.

Why now, of all times, had she shown up? The one person who could pull that rug out from underneath his confidence. Bridget seemed so infuriatingly successful, and yet so wounded. It bothered him immensely that that Anders fellow had stomped all over her huge capacity to love. Her great big heart was what surely made her a great nurse. It was one of the things that had stolen his heart. It bugged him that she would now be caring for all these people, right in front of him. But not caring *for* him.

Oh, medically she'd do whatever was necessary should he get hurt. But watching her lean over and say something to Dana that made them both laugh, Carson noticed the embers of old feelings resurfacing. *You can't go there.* "There" was exactly what Bridget had forbidden. In no uncertain terms. Besides, he was in no hurry to throw himself into Arthur Nicholson's crosshairs anytime soon.

He was trying to drag his gaze off Bridget when he sensed Mason coming up beside him. "You sure you're going to be okay with this?"

"Sure. Why?"

Mason raised one eyebrow. "You're staring."

Carson attempted denial. "Just watching."

Mason gave a grunt. "No, you're not. And you haven't been. Hey, look, I think she's a great fit for the camp, and we could sure use the help, but she's not the only nurse in Arizona. There are temp agencies we can tap for this sort of thing. We need to keep things on a professional level here. If that presents too much of a challenge…"

Carson raised a hand. "That's the newlywed in you talking. I've got it under control. *We've* got it under control." He caught his gaze straying back to Bridget, now tossing her hair in that way he'd always remembered her doing.

"Well, now, there you go," Mason said.

Mason's amused tone made Carson turn to his boss. "What?"

"At least you admit there's an 'it.'"

"*It's* not a problem." Carson emphasized the word.

"I'll hold you to that. And hope you'll come to me if that changes. In the meantime, I've got a project for you."

A project sounded like just what he needed— something to dig into for the weeks Bridget would be invading his thoughts. "What's up?"

"Dana's been talking with the counselors about ways families can do something positive in honor of their lost loved ones. A way to leave a permanent marker of their time here."

"What did you have in mind?"

Mason pointed out behind the house. "Trees. We could plant them on the grounds, or at the nature center, or anywhere they are needed. Something growing and living."

"What about a memorial garden? I've seen those. They can be beautiful. We can even do paving stones with names on them. Or things the kids can build."

Mason nodded. "See? That's why you're the right guy for the job. You get what we're trying to do here."

He did. People could say whatever they liked about the decidedly unswanky nature of his job here—he knew it was important. He was part of significant work, and he relished the way that sunk into his bones when he fell asleep tired at the end of every day.

"Do you want me to look into suppliers? Maybe someone in Phoenix if we can't find someone local?" Bridget laughed again and Carson fought to keep his focus on Mason and the new project. Maybe he didn't have it completely under control.

"I was hoping you'd say that. Let me know what you find." Mason squinted at the low sun and checked his watch. "And check into those circuit breakers again for me, will you? We blew a fuse in the big house again this morning."

Carson set his jaw. "Second time this week."

Some days it felt as if the camp utility systems were trying to outsmart him.

"Old houses can get cranky. We'll need to stay on top of it. The first families should be arriving in about an hour." He pulled in a deep breath. "Our first full season is about to start. I can't believe we're finally here."

Carson smiled. "I can." He couldn't think of any other people more meant to do what Mason, Dana and even Charlie were about to do. What all of the staff was about to do. He put a supportive hand on Mason's shoulder. "You're about to change some lives, boss."

"Maybe, but we've got to settle them in and feed them first. I'd better go check in with Seb to make sure that dinner will be ready." The staff ate dinner with all the families, gathered around enormous tables Mason had built to encourage everyone to get to know each other. So many little details of the camp were crafted to help each family reach out to others, to remove the isolation such a tragedy could often force on them.

Carson looked at the gate at the far end of the camp drive, now swung open in the welcome they were all preparing to give.

Here we go, Lord. Show up and stay close. To all of us.

Chapter Three

They all looked so weary.

As the families climbed down the steps of the little yellow bus, their battle-worn faces touched Bridget's heart. Whether a long flight or simply the two-hour drive from Phoenix, their expressions looked beyond tired.

"You're here!" the volunteer bus driver everyone called Busketeer Bart proclaimed. "Take a deep breath—you've made it."

"God bless our Busketeers," Dana said as she made her way to help the three families unload. The Busketeers were a group of older gentlemen who had taken up a mission to drive North Springs' school buses. The band of charming do-gooders became Camp True North Springs' transportation fleet in the summertime. They volunteered both behind the wheel and in dozens of other ways—Buske-teer fundraising breakfasts down at the town gazebo were legendary.

"Drink up!" Bridget called to the families as she waved hello. She'd made sure to stock the bus bringing families today with plenty of water. "It'll help with the altitude. And drink the ones in your rooms before dinner." She smiled at a little girl who offered a shy wave. "You, too, okay? Getting you hydrated today is just as important as settling you in."

"Welcome to Camp True North Springs," Mason said with his hands spread wide. "We're so glad you're here."

They did all seem happy to be among the beauty of the mountains. Many of them wore an awestruck expression she recognized. North Springs—and this wide-open corner of it, es-pecially—was a breathtaking place.

Dana had reminded the whole staff last night how that natural splendor made much of the healing possible. "A wounded soul needs re-minding that beauty is still in the world. God's creation has stood—and will stand—for years beyond our imagining." She'd blushed and laughed at such a poetic declaration, but ev-eryone had agreed it was true.

I want it to be true for me, too, if that's okay,

Lord, Bridget prayed as she helped a father pull suitcases from the bus. Even without the background files Dana had given her, Bridget could see that life had dealt these families hard blows. It was as if grief left a visible hole. A loss of light behind the eyes, a pressing down of shoulders, a resigned set of a jaw—so many details spoke of weariness and sorrow.

"Welcome, Nancy." Dana offered a hand to a petite woman with wavy blond hair. She hunched down to say hello to the little girl Bridget had reminded about the water. "I expect that makes you Polly." The girl nodded. "And Leo," she said to the slightly older boy next to her.

Nancy Michaels and her children had been a firefighter's family. The arsonist's blaze had been set to harm as many firefighters as possible, and Roger Michaels had perished alongside three of his colleagues.

Bridget could tell the woman who slowly limped her way down the bus steps was Adele Nunez. Adele had been delivering her premature daughter, Carla, in the back of an ambulance rushing to the hospital. A drunk driver had struck the vehicle so hard it rolled off the highway. Tiny Carla had survived a handful of days, but eventually succumbed to her injuries. Adele still had two more surgeries to heal her leg, but no medicine treated the lost look in her eyes. Adele's husband, Jim, carried a sleeping boy named Sammy against his shoulder while Mason helped Adele down the remaining steps.

Last off the bus was Doug Jennings. He corralled his three children with an admirable efficiency for a newly single father. He'd lost his wife not half a year ago when a senseless young man had opened fire in their grocery store.

A dose of the perspective she'd hoped to find up here on the mountain dropped itself into her chest with a resounding force: *And here I thought the end of my relationship with Anders was a tragedy.* It wasn't. People coping with real tragedies were standing in front of her. Her breakup with Anders only felt like a tragedy, and she could change that. God was already changing that. Bridget pulled in a deep breath, newly certain that her time here would indeed reframe what had happened on the *Brilliance.*

Little Missy Jennings walked up and held out her thumb with an adorable pout. "I squashed it."

Her father came up behind her with an apologetic smile. "She caught it on the zipper of her suitcase."

"Can I have a Band-Aid?" the little girl asked.

My first patient, Bridget thought with a smile. "Of course." Bridget knew even the smallest ouchies could be big to kids. Being able to ease this little girl's day lodged deep in Bridget's heart. "I've got lots to choose from." She looked up at the father, who was still keeping track of Missy's two brothers, Rob and John. The man certainly had his hands full. "I can take her back to the infirmary to treat her, then bring her to your room, or you can come with me. Whichever makes you more comfortable."

He gave an appreciative smile. "Go pick one out, Missy, and let—" he peered at Bridget's name badge "—Nurse Bridget bring you to our room when you're done."

Bridget extended a hand to the little girl, pleased when the child took it. Together they walked back to the infirmary, where Bridget lifted her up onto the exam table.

"First things first." Bridget pointed to the small bottle of water the child carried. "Take four good gulps. You need to drink a lot today and tomorrow."

Bridget peered at the reddened thumb while

the child complied. She turned the tiny thumb over in her expert hands, looking to see if the skin had been broken anywhere. "Does it hurt?"

"If I poke it." Missy looked around the office, swinging her chubby legs as they dangled off the table. "Do you live here?"

"For now. I'm just here until the permanent nurse comes."

Missy scrunched up her face and pulled her thumb close. "So you're not a real nurse?"

Bridget laughed. "I'm a very real nurse. I'm just not here for a very long time." She pulled the jar of brightly colored cartoon-character bandages from a nearby shelf. "And I'm extra good at little-girl bandages. Bunny, kitty or something else?"

"Bunny!" Missy held up her finger, then watched carefully as Bridget applied the bandage. After wiggling the newly bandaged finger to ensure it was in full working order, she looked at Bridget. "Who went away for you?"

It took a moment to realize what the girl was asking. Ashamed she could only answer, "No one," she added, "I'm here to help. I'm sorry your mama went away. That's very sad." She remembered Dana and Mason's instructions to encourage any camper to talk freely about the person they had lost. "What was your mom like?"

The little girl brightened. "She sang songs and made banana bread and liked the birds. We feed them. Bird food, not banana bread." Her giggle was sweet.

"She sounds wonderful. I'm glad you told me those things." Bridget helped Missy off the table and handed back the water bottle. "Two more gulps, please."

After she drank, Missy surprised Bridget by planting a kiss on her newly bandaged finger. "Mom used to do that. I don't know if it works without her."

Bridget's heart twisted in sympathy. She longed to make it all better, to restore all this little girl had lost. She couldn't, but perhaps she could fill in some of the gaps. "You know, nurse kisses have extra-special healing powers. I'll give your finger a superspecial Nurse Bridget kiss if you think it will help."

Missy considered the offer then gave a nod. "Okay." She held up her finger.

Bridget planted what she hoped was a super-special kiss onto the bunny bandage on Missy's finger. What would the medical staff of the *Brilliance* think of that protocol?

Missy wiggled her finger again. "It worked."

Not her mom's, but close enough. The girl's grin was all the affirmation Bridget needed. If anyone on the *Brilliance* medical staff might have taken issue with her improvised treatment, she refused to care.

"Can I go see my room now?" Missy asked.

"Absolutely. And then I'll see you again at dinner after you've unpacked. I hear Chef Seb makes amazing tacos, so bring your appetite— and a second empty water bottle."

As they walked toward the door, Missy grabbed Bridget's hand and planted a squishy kiss there. "Trade ya."

Very little in Bridget's life would be improved by a "kiss it and make it better" strategy. But given the glow Bridget felt in her chest, and the tiny spark of new purpose it seemed to signal, it was a nice start.

"Park your car over there by that building, and I'll help you with your bags," Carson told the older couple that had just driven up. Daniel and Sara Lohan were one of two families arriving in their own cars. Daniel and Sara were different than other camp families with young children. They had lost their only son, twenty-two-year-old Tom, when he was killed attempting to defend the safety of a young woman at a concert. Carson couldn't imagine what it would be like to have a family shattered like that, to no longer be a parent to a child you'd loved for over two decades.

"They're still parents," Dana had corrected him. "You never stop being a parent, even when your child is taken from you. I want us all to refer to Daniel and Sara as a family like every other family here."

For someone who continually reminded everyone she didn't have a counseling degree, Carson found Dana to be one of the most insightful and compassionate people he'd ever met. It wasn't hard to see why Mason had fallen so hard for her. Together, they were the perfect partnership to do what Camp True North Springs set out to do. *I'm grateful to be part of this, Lord*, Carson thought, *even if it's going to be sticky for a while with Bridget here*.

Carson fought the urge to raise a dubious eyebrow heavenward as Bridget walked toward him after delivering Missy to her room. The two of them were left standing in the yard. He hoped it would get easier to be anywhere alone with her—it certainly wasn't now.

She stared after the families now filing into

the house. "How do we do this? Help them when they all look so sad and tired?"

"Just what you did." When Bridget replied with a quizzical look, he continued, "You made one thing just a little bit better. And then another little thing, and then they laugh or smile and get a little bit stronger or happier or whatever it is they need to be."

Bridget shrugged. "It was just a bandage."

"That was more than a bandage. You have to know that. In fact, I expect you'll do more for these families in the weeks you're here than I will all summer. I just make sure things work right. You're tending to—" suddenly he couldn't think of how to explain it "—real needs. Aches, pains, minor emergencies, that sort of thing."

"Let's hope all the emergencies are minor. Better yet, no emergencies at all. Especially with Matteo." Bridget looked at the gate. "They should be here by now. I hope everything's okay."

"The Lohans told me highway traffic was bad. Maybe they got stuck."

Bridget sighed. "I just hope we can keep him healthy while he's here. Martina says the early months of remission can be tricky. A little emergency can turn into a big one with a post-chemo patient like Matteo. I've been reading up on pediatric leukemia, and it sounds like a long uphill climb."

Of course, Bridget had already done extensive research on Matteo's behalf. She'd been full of compassion, and a rough patch didn't take that away from some people. In fact, he was pretty sure hard times made compassionate people even more compassionate.

"So he's over it? That's why they're coming?"

"He's in remission. For now. If it comes back—and evidently it does a lot of the time—things get more serious. Martina said it's likely the real solution would be a bone marrow transplant."

"That sounds serious," Carson replied.

Bridget hugged her chest and frowned. "It is. They basically wipe out all his immunity and start from scratch with healthy cells from someone else." She looked at Carson with concern in her eyes. "It's risky stuff. It doesn't always work. I can't imagine living with that hanging over your head."

He had to agree. "And on top of all the grief of losing her husband in combat." It didn't seem fair. Then again, nothing that had happened to any of the families he'd met today seemed fair. Mason was right when he'd said that Camp True North Springs' number one foe wasn't logistics or nature, it was despair.

"She's *our age*, Carson. And she's already gone through all that. How on earth do we help someone facing so much?" She shot Carson a dubious look. "And don't say a bunny Band-Aid. What Martina needs is way beyond anything I can give her."

He'd had much the same burst of doubt an hour ago. What they were trying to do here seemed to be an act of monumental faith. Still, he'd seen the happiness Dana and Mason and Charlie now carried. Even Chef Seb and his fiancée, Kate, bore witness to what the camp could do to restore some hope.

She needed a boost, but Carson couldn't say something too personal like, "I have faith in you."

"What's the biggest emergency you handled on the ship?" He made a point of using the correct term in his question.

"Three heart attacks, one appendicitis attack and an impressive collection of broken bones."

"No delivering babies?"

He said that to make her laugh, and it did. "The cruise line didn't permit women that far along in their pregnancies to sail. And we had three doctors for the serious stuff."

"And we have the medical center," he reminded her. "Your job isn't to cure Matteo's cancer. Your job is to help him be safe and fun while he's here."

"But so many things could go wrong. What if something goes wrong?"

"You call the ambulance and keep things under control until the paramedics get here."

She shot him a sideways glance. "You make it sound like anyone could do my job."

"Oh, no," he replied, glad she'd finally given him an opportunity to praise her. "You're just the person for the job. You care in just the right way, and I've seen the bunny Band-Aids to prove it. You'll make all the little adjustments and bits of care happen. You'll make Martina's and Matteo's stay here possible. Everyone's, when you think about it." He knew he was probably going too far, but he wanted to say it and she seemed to need to hear it. "Your being here gives these moms and dads one less thing to worry about. I can't help but think what a huge gift that is."

Her slight smile went straight to his heart. "You always were good at pep talks."

He leaned in just a bit. "Anytime you need one, you know where to find me."

Carson knew that had gone one step too far the minute he'd said the words. Bridget's palms rose to form a gesture that said "keep your distance," whether she'd intentionally meant it or not. She stepped back. "I'll be fine. I'll do some more research, talk to Martina when she gets here, and I'll be fine." She seemed ashamed to be caught admitting her earlier doubts, to let him see that tender part of her. Her "Nurse Bridget in Control" voice had returned.

"I just want you to know…" He wasn't sure how to say what he was thinking—or if he should say it at all. "I don't think it's any mistake that they're coming. Or that you're here."

The breeze tossed Bridget's hair and she swiped the locks out of her eyes to stare at him. "What?"

"Things are lining up. She's here, she thought of you, you were available, Matteo's remission lets him be here…" His words fell off and he shrugged. "God stuff, don't you think?"

"Maybe."

"So maybe you can trust that it's all going to work out."

"Maybe." Her shoulders straightened a bit at that. "Yeah, maybe." After an awkward moment, she said, "I should check on a few things. Keep an eye out for their car, will you?"

As he watched Bridget head back toward the guest quarters, the sound of footsteps made Carson turn toward the woodshop behind him.

"Nicely done," Mason said, pulling a set of work gloves off his hands and stuffing them in his jeans' pockets. "I wasn't eavesdropping, but an open window lets in more than the breeze."

Carson shook his head. "This is gonna be hard. We were so close once. I don't know where to draw the line now. And I keep tripping over it, you know?"

Mason looked at him. "Did you just hear yourself?"

"Spouting a lot of words?" Carson winced. Sometimes his mouth and his nonstop urge to fix anything that looked broken got him into a world of trouble.

"Talking about how things are lining up," Mason corrected. "Everyone who is here is supposed to be here. God's at work. Has been from the very beginning. That means however you and Bridget work things out has to be part of that plan, too."

Carson wanted to gulp at that thought. Half in hope that maybe, somehow, they could create a less agonizing relationship between them—and half that this would put a permanent cap of closure on their painful past.

Chapter Four

Just over an hour later, a pair of adorable brown eyes looked up at Bridget from under a bright green baseball cap. "Hi!" Chubby fingers wiggled in a cheerful wave.

The woman Bridget recognized as Martina Garza put a tender hand on her son's shoulder. "Matteo, this is Nurse Bridget. She's an old friend of Mommy's."

"Hello, Matteo, it's nice to meet you." She tried not to stare at the baby-fine soft brown hair that peeked out from under the cap. Had his hair once been as thick as his mother's wavy locks? In every other way, he looked like a garden-variety rambunctious preschool boy. "You'll have fun here," she said with confidence. All the staff would do everything they could to make sure that was true.

Matteo looked around. "Are there lizards?"

Garden-variety little boy indeed. The total lack of fear in the boy's question amused Bridget. "Lots of 'em."

Martina did not share her son's fascination. "He's been very excited to see lizards," she lamented. "We don't have them in Milwaukee. I was content to leave them in Arizona."

Bridget laughed and gave Martina a smile. "They're not my favorite, either. I've been around the world and seen all kinds of critters, but I still shrieked when one crawled across my shoe the other night."

Martina gave an envious sigh. "I want to hear about those travels. It sounds wonderful." Then, as if she remembered how those travels had come to an end, her face darkened.

Matteo tugged on his mother's arm. "Mama, it's hot." His tone reminded Bridget that the garden-variety preschooler also came with a lot of whining.

"The heat is why lizards like it here so much," Bridget explained. "And it's why you need to drink all this water." She handed over two water bottles. "Drink lots for the first few days, okay?" She unscrewed the cap on the smaller one and handed it to Matteo. "Especially you. Every time I see you, I'm going to check your water bottle. Got it?"

"Can I have lemonade?" he asked. Matteo looked as if he knew exactly how persuasive those big brown eyes could be.

"After you drink your water," she replied with a wink. She returned her gaze to Martina. "How was the drive?" She'd flown into Scottsdale to spend a week with her parents who lived there now, then had driven here to the camp.

Martina rolled her shoulders and winced. "Long. I'm glad I wasn't foolish enough to try driving all the way from Milwaukee. Four-year-olds just aren't built for long-distance travel." She leaned in toward Bridget. "I played some videos so much I hope I never see them again."

Bridget could only imagine what it took to keep a boy like Matteo occupied on such a long trip. "There's a lot to do around here, and all kinds of new friends to make. Charlie has volunteered to be Matteo's honorary big brother for his time here, and you can't do better than that."

"Mason and Dana's son? Really?" Martina seemed touched.

"I get a brother while I'm here?" Matteo's

excitement was bittersweet. Considering how recently Martina had been widowed, life wouldn't hand Matteo another sibling anytime soon. But hopefully someday, since Martina struck Bridget as the kind of person who'd want a big family.

"You sure do. Charlie's great. And he knows all about lizards."

And what it's like to lose a parent so young, Bridget thought. Sure, her own dreams had been shut down when her engagement to Anders had ended, but not in the huge way that Martina's life had been altered. To be a widowed mother at that age? It seemed hard on so many levels. It would help so much for Martina and Matteo to be with other people who'd been through the same kinds of loss.

"Is there anything I should know about what Matteo needs while he's here?" Martina had emailed a list of Matteo's medications as well as a daunting list of his specialists and oncologists should something go wrong. Definitely far beyond bunny Band-Aids.

"Not unless we end up with shenanigans."

Bridget raised an eyebrow. "Shenanigans?"

"That's what Matteo's team at the hospital calls complications." She offered a hopeful smile. "We've been shenanigan-free for eight weeks. I'm hoping we keep it that way. If we get to six months post-chemo without shenanigans, we get to say he's officially in remission."

"And hair," Matteo said. His near-bald status didn't seem to faze him. He yanked off his hat to show the light brown peach fuzz adorning his tawny brown scalp. "I'm just getting it back. Doctor Jay said it might even be a different color. I want green."

Bridget could only laugh. "Green? Like a lizard?" Dana had told her to be prepared to be astonished at the resilience of children. "Why not?"

"Because his mama is not sending him to kindergarten with green hair," Martina said in mock scolding tones. "Doctor Jay was teasing you."

Matteo planted the hat back on his head. "I'd like it."

Martina touched her son's chin with affection. "I'll just settle for hair. And no shenanigans."

"I bet it grows while you're here," Bridget offered. "Let me take a picture now, and we'll compare it with your last day. Would you like that?"

Matteo pulled the hat back off and offered a grin while Bridget got out her cell phone.

He grabbed his mother's hand and pulled her down so that they both could be in the picture. As she focused the shot, Bridget thought of what Carson had said. *Make one thing just a little bit better.* Nursing would go far beyond medical care in a place like this. She found the challenge of that deeply compelling. Perhaps Carson was right, and God really was lining things up in ways she was only beginning to understand.

The photo was charming. She turned her phone to show Martina and Matteo, warmed by the smiles on their faces. "I'll send you this. And I'll print one out so we can officially compare it to the one we take before you go back to Milwaukee. With more hair," she emphasized, daring to run a hand over the boy's fuzzy head. "Oh, that's so soft."

Matteo ducked and moaned. "Why do girls always want to touch my hair?"

Bridget gave him a smirk. "In a dozen years, you might think that's a good thing. Even better than lizards."

Matteo frowned in disbelief as the hat returned to his head. Bridget was glad for the laugh she and Martina shared. It felt good to make a long hard day a little bit lighter for her. "Let's get you and your bags in out of this heat.

I checked, and there's a fridge in your room. And a good stock of water bottles. Dinner's soon, too."

"Any snacks? I'm hungry now."

"Chef Seb—you'll meet him at dinner—keeps snacks out in the dining room all day. I promise you won't go hungry. But it's really close to time for tacos, and Chef Seb makes great ones."

"I love tacos!" the boy said. He looked up at his mom. "I like it here so far."

"Good," Bridget said as she accepted one of the many bags Martina was pulling from the back of the car. "That's the plan. For both of you."

The camp staff met every morning in the small conference room that sat just off the dining room in the big house. Carson didn't mind taking the empty chair next to Bridget at Saturday's meeting.

"Everyone settle in okay last night?" Mason asked from his place at the head of the conference table.

"So far, so good," Dana replied. She glanced over to Bridget. "Anyone having trouble with the altitude?" North Springs was significantly above sea level and not everyone handled the adjustment well, especially in the summer heat.

"Daniel and Sara were feeling it a bit this morning," Bridget reported. "But everyone else seems to be okay. We need to keep on everyone about the water for at least another twenty-four hours. And sunscreen. I've set a few bottles of adult and kid versions out in the common room just in case anyone forgot theirs."

Mason nodded his approval. "That's the kind of addition we've needed on the staff. Providing things for the families even before they need them."

"A bad sunburn can ruin anyone's stay, especially some of those little ones," Carson commented, offering a smile to Bridget.

Chef Seb came in late from breakfast, gulping down coffee as he sat. "Speaking of setting things out, I've made sure the water canister out by the snacks is full at all times. We'll nudge everyone to fill up on their way out from meals. I've been telling 'em, 'Don't let Nurse Bridget see you with an empty water bottle.'"

Bridget frowned. "You can't see through those bottles. I couldn't tell if one was empty."

Seb gave a mischievous smirk. "I may or may not have hinted that you have X-ray vision."

Her jaw dropped. "You didn't!"

Dana's look matched Bridget's. "We do not lie to children at Camp True North Springs."

Seb held up his hands. "Hey, I'm just messing with you. I just said don't let her catch you with an empty water bottle. But your faces just now? Totally worth it."

Bridget looked at Carson. "Is he always like this?"

"Pretty much. You get used to it."

They churned through a list of other tasks and issues, all with an eye toward giving the campers the best experience possible. When it came to Carson's turn, he opened a file and passed out a sheet of paper to each person. "Mason came to me with the idea of starting a memorial garden to pay tribute to the loved ones of everyone who comes here."

Bridget looked up from the paper. "Don't you already do that with the flowers on the pond?" Carson had told her about the extraordinary little ceremony families did at the end of their stay. Everyone sent a flower floating out across the camp's pond, a nod to the memorial practice of Mason's late wife and her Hawaiian heritage.

"That's true," Carson replied. "But this is something lasting and growing. Something they can know is still there and thriving years from now."

He motioned to the diagram of a winding stone path, the low brick wall with an arch, and the collection of trees and plants he had in mind for an area of the property that wasn't getting much use now. The ideas had begun flowing into his head the minute Mason had brought it up, and pride warmed his nervous spirit. Was he overstepping here? The garden was ambitious, and a bit beyond his abilities.

"Think about it," he went on. "All the future families can see the names of the families that came before them. It…" He paused a moment before adding, "I think it places them in the larger family of everyone who's gone through this. I have to think that's comforting. Maybe even a source of strength." He felt his face flush, as if he'd gone too far in his enthusiasm.

Until he looked at Bridget. Her eyes held a sense of wonder. Awe even. As if she, in her endless supply of compassion, understood exactly what he was trying to say. In fact, the whole staff looked that way. Amazing smiles of encouragement came from everyone. His lingering doubts as to whether or not he belonged on the Camp True North Springs' staff melted away in the reaction of his colleagues.

Especially his boss. Mason looked more than pleased. "This is far beyond what I had in mind. I just figured we'd add a few plants, but you've turned it into something so much more. The bricks that can have names, the pathway stones that can have names, the way it can be a place to come sit and think and remember? Carson, this is fabulous."

"It's just masonry and a few plantings." Carson backtracked. "Simple stuff, but we can add to it with each camp session."

"It's a wonderful plan," Mason declared. "Get started." He looked around the table. "Anything else to cover today?"

Carson sensed Bridget straightening in the seat next to him. "Actually, I have an idea I'd like to pose." She cleared her throat. "If it's okay?"

"Absolutely," Dana said.

"Martina happened to mention a need she's struggling with for Matteo. I think we can help. I know these families are here to heal, but part of that healing could be in how they help each other."

"I certainly like the sound of that," Mason replied.

"What have you got in mind?" Carson asked, trying to put a similar supportive tone in his voice that Mason seemed to have mastered. He so admired how the man made everyone feel as if each person was able to contribute. The fact that Bridget had already proposed an idea showed just what a good leader Mason proved to be. No one felt afraid to pose even the craziest of ideas here, even in their first days.

Bridget spread her hands across the table in front of her. "Matteo is in early remission. That means he's at a place where he can consider a bone marrow transplant. It could be a cure, not just ongoing management. Only he needs a donor, and Martina isn't a match."

"Wouldn't she have to be?" Seb asked. "She's his mom."

"It doesn't always work that way. And with his dad gone, and no siblings, he'll need to find a donor from the general public, where the odds are much harder." She met the eyes of several of the staff as she talked. "I think we could try to help find that for him. We could do a bone marrow donor drive."

"How would we do that all the way out here?" Dana asked.

"I did some research. It's a simple test, no needles or anything like that. A cheek swab and you sign yourself onto a registry. A match could save a life."

"Are we enough people to do any good?" Dana asked. "None of us have any relation to his family."

"That's true, but we can get the families—only if they want to, of course—and us, and maybe people down in North Springs. After all, Martina and her parents used to live here. If we get just one match out of the whole drive, even if it's not for Matteo, I have to think it will make a difference. I'm going to do it no matter what, but I think we all could do it."

Mason looked at Dana. "The Busketeers would be all over this. We could ask them to help. Maybe host one of their pancake breakfasts for it."

"And the church," Seb suggested. "We could get a load of people that way."

"What do you think?" Bridget asked.

Heads nodded all around the table. "Full speed ahead on both projects," Mason declared. "But—" he held up a hand "—let's be extra careful we don't overwhelm Martina or any of the families. If we get any sense this is too much while they're here to heal, we back off. Agreed?"

"Agreed," was the universal response.

Bridget looked at Carson with a spark of excitement lighting her eyes. He knew what a powerhouse she could be when she set her mind to something. It was going to be an adventure to watch her idea unfold. And now he was unfolding his own idea, as well.

Mason caught Carson's arm on the way out of the meeting. "Got a minute?"

"Sure, boss."

"Gordon Jacobs said something when he was here fixing the circuit breakers yesterday."

It had bothered Carson that he couldn't fix the problem and they'd had to call in an expensive electrician. "That I need to be more careful when I plug in more than four pieces of equipment in the workshop?" He was only half joking.

"That the camp could benefit from having a licensed electrician on-site."

The camp couldn't afford a two-person maintenance staff. They could barely afford to bring the nurse on for this session, and Dana had said they'd need a third counselor soon. "The system is finicky, that's for sure, but you don't have that kind of money, do you?"

"He meant you, Carson. Gordon wants to know if you're interested in trade school or an apprenticeship."

"School? Not my thing." Never had been. One of the things he liked most about Camp

True North Springs was that no one seemed to be shoving him toward self-improvement here. Didn't anyone understand he was content the way he was? "I don't think so. Not now, at least."

"I thought I should ask. Gordon thinks highly of you."

Carson didn't like the way the compliment sat expectantly on his shoulders. "Good to know. But I'm not interested." Expectations could become oppressive things—he'd learned that a long time ago.

Chapter Five

The rest of the weekend went by with only minor nursing needs. On Monday, little Sammy Nunez came in with an angry knee scrape he had acquired taking a tumble over some rocks.

After a stint of Nurse Bridget TLC, Sammy gaped down at his wound then up at Bridget. "It didn't sting!"

Bridget sat back and crossed her arms over her chest. "Told ya." She'd had a battle to let the boy allow her to disinfect his knee.

Sammy's mother, Adele, shifted off her bad leg and leaned against the counter. "My mother-in-law used an alcohol pad on one of Sammy's cuts while I was in the hospital, and now he's sure everything will hurt like that."

Straight isopropyl alcohol? On a child's cut?

Bridget winced. "Ouch indeed. Nothing you get in here will hurt like that, I promise." She pointed toward the cleaned wound. "How many Band-Aids?"

It really only needed one, but sometimes a child's count told her a lot. It was the Camp True North Springs' version of asking the cruise patrons if they needed more than a few Tylenol—the response was always telling. And often had little to do with the injury at hand.

Sammy assessed his knee with pint-size seriousness. "Two."

"Two it is." Bridget reached for the jar that had already become her trademark. It was a rather nice thing to be known for Band-Aids and ice packs rather than the *Brilliance*'s complicated adult problems. No one here had eaten exotic fish or spent too much time at the ship's bar or overestimated their skills off the pool diving board. The simple joys of bumps, boo-boos and Band-Aids made a nice counterbalance to the graver problems of kids like Matteo.

As she applied the first Band-Aid—a green one with fish—Bridget asked Adele, "How did that hip do on yesterday's hike? Hold up okay?" Despite her pronounced limp from the accident, Adele had insisted on joining Sammy and her husband, Jim, on a short Sunday afternoon hike up the mountain.

"I held on to Jim half the time," Adele admitted, rubbing her side. "And I'm sore. But I'm glad I went."

"Dad says Mom's a trouper," Sammy offered as Bridget finished off the second bandage—blue with frogs. "But I think she was a hopper. Like Franco out front." Sammy squished up his face. "He spit water at me when I fell."

"I suppose I did hop a bit," Adele said, laughing. "It was steeper than I thought up there."

"Maybe a little ice tonight? And some ibuprofen? And a porch rocking chair while the boys build birdhouses?"

Adele's eyes lit up in mock horror. "I have a degree in architecture. No way am I missing birdhouse building." She grinned at her son, who was swinging his leg off the exam table as if to check that his knee still worked. "We know that girls build things, too, don't they?"

"Sure do." Sammy's nod was adorable.

Bridget finished with the bandage wrappers and then handed Adele a reusable ice pack. "This should help." She couldn't help but smile as mother and son walked off hand in hand, each favoring opposite legs.

She leaned out the infirmary door to watch them turn the corner into the common room, finding the pair a perfect picture of the camp's purpose—people with hurts helping others with hurts walk a little farther along. *I'm glad to be here.*

"Look at you grinning." Carson's voice came from the opposite side of the room. When she turned in his direction, she found him leaning against the bookcases, toolbox in hand and an amused look on his face. "It's nice," he added softly, as if he wasn't sure it was okay to say that.

She wasn't sure it was okay to say that, especially with the warm tone in his voice. "Some of these kids are so sweet, it breaks your heart."

"Some of these kids are so strong, it blows you away." He walked toward her. "The oldest Jennings boy? John? He told me he wanted to become a police officer so he could protect people because he knows it would make his mom proud." Carson shook his head. "Got a lump in my throat on that one. Some guy shoots your mom down in a grocery store and you want to be the guy who stops the next one. Who has that kind of conviction at twelve? I think I wanted to be a football player at that age."

"Makes a kind of sense to me. If your life's been toppled by one of the bad guys, you want to be one of the good guys." She dared bringing up something from her past with him. "You remember how Grandma's illness started me wanting to be a nurse."

"That's different," Carson said.

"Not really," Bridget replied.

Carson walked over and put his tool case down on the table next to where Bridget was standing. "You being a nurse didn't put you on the front line to get sick like your grandmother. I can tell how John's idea socks his father, Doug, in the gut. The last thing he needs is another member of his family gunned down."

Bridget let out a sigh. "I hadn't thought of it that way. But John's still young. He has time to find a dozen different roads in life."

"That's a bit funny coming from you," Carson remarked, a bit of an edge replacing the earlier warmth in his tone.

"Meaning what?"

"You knew where you wanted to go in life and headed straight for it. I don't remember you being too keen on my taking my time to find different roads in life."

Here was one of those pitfalls left by their history. Bridget supposed it was inevitable that they tripped over a few of these old tensions. "You were in your twenties. John is half that age." She decided to be bold and ask, "Why didn't you ever go to college?"

Carson bristled immediately. "Is that you or your father asking?"

She replied with a dark look. "Me. I know you did a lot of wandering around. You never did tell me how you ended up here."

Defensiveness narrowed his eyes. "I *did* do a lot of wandering. And just because it wasn't on some shiny boat on Dad's dime does not mean it was a waste of time."

Where was this coming from? "I never said you were wasting time. I wanted to know what brought you here. What you did with yourself since…" She suddenly found it hard to finish that sentence.

"Since you left here, left me," he finished for her. "I bounced around a lot—wherever my angry, hurt self felt like going. I'd stay in town for a bit until it got too hard, then go off somewhere. Nowhere in particular. So, yes, you could say I did a lot of wandering around."

Carson ran his hand across the handle of the toolbox. "Mom and Dad would make suggestions sometimes. About school or careers. I ignored them and took various odd jobs fixing things. And found out I'm good at that. Probably not your fancy definition of purpose, but it is mine."

"So you started fixing things here?"

"Mason needed help even before Dana came to him about the camp. I'd tackle some jobs for him now and then. Once the idea for the camp took hold, there was a lot to do. So I started doing more and more until he offered me a job. So if you're asking how I got here, that's how. No fancy school or training, just common sense and wanting to help." He paused before adding, "We're making a difference here."

Bridget felt the purpose in his words tug at her heart. So many people cared so much here. How could it not make a difference? "You are," she said, glad to see the affirmation ease the friction that had risen up between them. She surprised herself by needing to stifle the urge to reach out and touch his arm.

Carson straightened, picking his toolbox back up. "I was coming to ask if you wanted a ride into town. Mason said you were going this afternoon."

After momentarily thinking it wasn't a good idea, Bridget changed her mind. "That'd help, yes."

Carson looked surprised. "Help?"

"I'm going into town to talk to Bart Salinas about getting the Busketeers involved in the bone marrow drive. And maybe talk to Dad." She'd worked out how she might try to have another conversation with Dad about both the camp and her donor drive idea today. It would help if she went with Bart's approval in her pocket. People listened to Dad. Most people considered him a pillar of the community, and he was involved in dozens of projects he felt preserved the unique character of North Springs. He'd been asked to run for mayor twice, but declined each time, saying he preferred to stick to his role as businessman and chair of the zoning board. "It'll be so much easier to get everyone else on board with the drive if I could get Dad behind it."

Carson's opinion of Dad showed all over his face. Mostly because Dad made no secret of his opinion of Carson as too poor and unambitious to deserve his daughter. "Long shot," he declared darkly.

"I know. But I'm going to try."

Hannah Young came out from behind the counter at the grocery store with her usual friendly smile. "Hey, Carson. How's the first official session going up there on the mountain?"

"Good so far. 'Course it's only been a couple of days." Carson sighed. "The stories never cease to get you, you know?"

Hannah looked out the store's front window in the direction of the mountains. "I can only imagine. I admit, half of me wasn't sure Dana would pull it off. Not that I doubted her—it was mostly her ability to convince Mason. Then again, I don't think any of us thought it'd turn into such a love story."

"Yeah, they're newlyweds, all right." He'd been a bit worried at first, how all that happiness would play out right next to all those grieving families. Turns out, it made for a hopeful counterbalance. Much the way the younger ones could play and laugh—it reminded everyone that happiness wasn't totally gone from the world.

"What can I do for you?"

"I need a candy bar."

Hannah started walking toward that aisle in the store. "I've got lots of them—pick your favorite."

"Well, that's just the thing," Carson said, suddenly finding his idea ridiculous. "It's not for me. I need to guess a person's favorite."

"Hmm." Hannah's eyebrows arched. "Do I know this person?"

"Maybe," was the best answer Carson could come up with.

The grocer began running her hand down the aisle of candy the way a librarian would run a hand down a shelf of books. "Male or female?"

"Um…female."

Carson immediately regretted the knowing glint in Hannah's eyes. "Figured. In my experience, guys don't buy sweets for other guys." She stopped her hand's wandering to look at him squarely. "Is this happy chocolate or coping chocolate?"

"How can you be sure it's chocolate?"

"Let's just say the odds are highly in favor of chocolate. Unless it's your boss, Dana, in which case you need to be over at Guerro's buying a vat of queso. She's a rare cheese gal. In all other situations, you want to go with chocolate. So, happy or coping?"

Carson thought of the possible scenarios. If Bridget only spoke with Bart and Rita Salinas, it'd be happy chocolate. But given Rita's skill and fondness for baked goods, any good conversation over at the Gingham Pocket bed-and-breakfast probably ended with sweets. No, he was here for the other outcome: that Bridget had gotten brave enough to go visit her father.

He didn't see any way that could end well. "Probably coping." After a second, he added, "Lots of coping. But I can't look like I'm trying too hard."

"That's a lot to ask of a chocolate bar. But if you need to walk a fine line, it's a better choice than a box of chocolates or something like that. And ice cream is out of the question in this heat." She tapped a finger against her chin as she considered the selection in front of them. "Are you going to give me a name?"

"Nope." Bridget would have his hide if he let anyone know what he was doing.

Reaching out, Carson pulled a pack of peanut butter cups from the shelf.

"Choosing on your own, huh?" Hannah asked. "Brave."

"These are for me. It looks better if we both have something, right?"

She nodded. "Good thinking. I'm going to suggest the king-size chocolate-and-caramel bar." She grabbed it and the larger size package of the peanut butter cups he'd passed over. "Upsize yourself, too, so she doesn't feel guilty."

This wasn't supposed to be so complicated. "I just want to do something nice for a friend."

"Friend?" Hannah practically winked.

"Friend," Carson repeated. Bridget's preference for friendship was starting to bother him. Old feelings were stubbornly rising up despite the bouts of awkwardness between them.

Walking to the cash register, Hannah rang up the sale. "The world needs more friends like you." She stopped, suddenly darting back to the aisle. "How about I throw in a couple of bags of licorice for the kids up at camp? On me? Besides, this way it looks like you just had a quick thought while you were in here for licorice. See what I did there?"

Carson handed over the cash for the pair of candy bars. "The world needs more people like you, Hannah. Thanks."

His casual call of farewell died in his throat as he caught sight of Bridget. She sat with slumped shoulders in the town square gazebo. It looked like she *had* gone to see her dad and it'd gone as badly as he predicted.

Carson carefully mounted the small set of steps into the gazebo and sat a slight distance away from her. "You saw your dad."

She sniffed, sighed and rolled her eyes. "I don't know what I thought would happen. It's not like I expected that he'd suddenly get behind anything involving the camp. Only, this isn't the camp. It's one little boy and anyone else we might end up helping. Honestly, Carson, who could be against that?"

Carson remained silent. Without a word, he pulled the large caramel-and-chocolate bar from the bag and slid it across the bench toward her. "I figured you might need a little cheering up. Or it was just an excuse to get my own. Pick your motive." He waved the peanut butter cups at her with a playful grin.

She laughed, a damp sort of laugh that let him know she was trying not to cry. It cut through to his heart and made him want to go give Arthur Nicholson a piece of his mind. That man was just plain mean. "Did you talk about the camp?"

She shook her head. "Oh, I didn't even try that topic. But I got an earful, anyway. He's dead set against it, so sure all those 'unfortunate people' will harm North Springs." She gave the term air quotes with her fingers at what had to be her father's awful choice of words.

Arthur probably took her employment there as a purposeful jab at the Nicholson family disapproval, which, actually, Carson thought it was. Not that he'd bring up that right now.

He settled for a neutral statement of fact. "So he was against the donor drive by association, huh?"

Bridget turned to look at him. "Instantly. I didn't even get the full explanation out before he practically shut me down. What has he got against the Garzas, anyway? It's no one's fault Matteo is sick. The way Dad talked, you'd think they'd done something to earn his illness. As if cancer or losing your dad at that age was some punishment you *deserved*."

There wasn't any attitude that flew in the face of the camp's mission more. Coping with the unfairness of it all, the injustice of the kinds of tragedies visited on these families, was the whole point of why Camp True North Springs brought them together. "That's harsh. And wrong." A lot more words piled up at the base of his throat, but he swallowed them back down. He was here to listen, to help get her over it so she could go back up the mountain and care for those very same families.

Bridget stood up. "Given all the stories I've heard this week, do you know how that galled me? I know Dad can be mean and judgmental, but this feels so…so…" She waved off finishing the sentence, choosing instead to sit back down and tear open the candy bar. She did it with such a relish that Carson reminded himself to thank Hannah for her excellent instincts next time he saw her.

She bit off a large piece and closed her eyes. "Oh. This is perfect," she moaned behind a mouthful of chocolate. She opened her eyes again, just the slightest hint of spark returning to them. "Unhealthy, poor coping skills, but absolutely perfect."

"It'll be our secret. Think of it as the grown-up version of bunny Band-Aids." She genuinely laughed at that, and Carson let her indulge for a moment before trying to steer the conversation elsewhere. "What about the Busketeers?"

She brightened immediately. "Oh, they're in. Bart thinks it's a great idea." She took another bite, and Carson enjoyed the satisfaction of knowing he'd helped her out of her dark mood. "They'll do one of their breakfasts to draw people out and even pick up folks who can't get in on their own. He wants the Busketeers to try for three hundred registrants. Maybe more."

"I wouldn't be surprised if you get more than three hundred. Maybe even five hundred. Think of all the good you could do with that even if we don't find a match for Matteo."

"Yeah," she said with less enthusiasm than he'd hoped. She had to know that North Springs was bigger than her father's look-down-your-nose attitude. *Show Bridget that,* he prayed, seeing the light fade from her eyes as she scanned across the town square to where her father's office was. *Cut down that long shadow Arthur has over her so she can be her own person.*

Hannah's words came back to him as they spent a few more moments eating their chocolate in the peace of the afternoon. *The world may need more Bridgets. But I'm beginning to need this one.*

Chapter Six

Dana showed no surprise when Bridget relayed the outcome of her conversations in town the next morning. "I never doubted for a minute Bart and Rita would be on board. Those Busketeers are a mighty force for good."

Bridget felt her chin stick out like a petulant child's. "Well, I'm not sure what kind of force Dad is. It's like we can't talk about anything anymore. Were things this bad between us before I left? Or am I just seeing it with new eyes?"

Dana tapped the stack of envelopes they had been sorting into a tidy square on the conference table. "Family can push our buttons in ways no one else can. Half the conflicts I tried to solve back in Denver had some seed in a family fight. They're supposed to be the ones that love us, and we get pulled up short when they don't."

"But what makes the violence show up in such ugly ways?"

Dana offered a soft look. "You're trying to make sense of something that won't ever make sense. In some cases, the violence is there because the tools of violence are there. Hurt people use whatever they've got—guns and knives in some cases, or money and power in others. I'm hoping what we do here gives them a new set of tools while the wounds heal. Stops the cycle, you know?"

Hurt people did use whatever weapons they had. Bridget thought of the cruise patron who had said the wrong thing to his brother-in-law with a shuffleboard puck nearby. The broken nose would heal, but Bridget doubted the relationship ever would. Dana was right about one thing—pain didn't seem to care about wealth or poverty. She'd seen respectable people behave terribly on the ship and yet, here at camp, Bridget saw people some might classify as underprivileged behave with incredible grace and valor. Why couldn't Dad see that?

"We don't need him, you know," Dana said as if she'd heard Bridget's thoughts. "We can do the drive without your dad. No offense, but

I think everything we accomplish despite his objections is a plus."

"None taken. I just thought…" There seemed little point in expressing her silly hope that this project would be the thing to turn him around. No one turned Dad around on anything.

"He'll just have to watch us succeed without him. Spectacularly." They walked out of the room and Dana deposited the stack of envelopes into the Outgoing Mail basket in the front hall. It joined an adorable collection of hand-colored postcards made by the families this morning. "I can't wait until we tell Martina and Matteo about the bone marrow donor drive. And the rest of the families. Your project and Carson's memorial gardens are just the kinds of things we need."

"How do you want to tell them?"

"You mean how do *you* want to tell them? It's your idea, you should get to announce it. Mason was thinking maybe at dinner—after you clear it all with Martina first, of course. Did you call the donor center to get out the details?"

"I've got a meeting set up. If Martina okays it, we'll pick a few dates for within this camp session and see which ones work best for the Busketeers."

"And if she doesn't?"

Bridget stilled. "I hadn't thought about that. I mean why wouldn't she?"

"Martina and Matteo are here to heal. Sometimes that means taking an empowering step forward. Sometimes it doesn't. I love your idea, really, but we need to respect Martina's call on this."

Bridget knew in her heart that Dana spoke the truth. "You're right. That's true."

"Healing doesn't always look like what we had planned." Bridget wondered if the woman realized her hand strayed to her abdomen as she spoke. Dana had been seriously wounded from a gunshot while on the Denver police force. Physically, she'd recovered from the shot, but her true healing came from creating Camp True North Springs. Bridget admired her courage in following the crazy dream that had brought her to Mason and Charlie's doorstep. Dana was a true inspiration, although she rarely accepted that term. Dana insisted she hadn't really had a choice; the idea and God had hounded her until she'd given in. And that had included doing battle with Arthur Nicholson—and winning—which made Bridget admire her even more.

"Still," Bridget insisted, "wouldn't it be incredible if we sent Matteo home with a bone marrow donor match?"

"It would. And you can be sure I'll be praying for that outcome. But you said it's an incredible long shot. So we need to be ready to accept whatever outcome we get, right?"

"Yes." Bridget wished her words had a more mature sense of perspective. Much like the way Dana described her initial call to create the camp, the idea of the donor drive had grabbed a hold of Bridget and refused to let go. *I need to get to the place where I won't feel like I've failed if we can't do it, or don't find a match.*

Dana put an arm around Bridget. "It's not unlike the thing with your dad, come to think of it."

Bridget didn't see the similarities at all. "How do you figure that?"

"You can try to smooth things over with him. And you should. For yourself, even more than for him. But you can't control how people react. If he doesn't come around—on this or on the camp—that's out of your hands. I had to figure out pretty early in all this that I'm responsible for my effort and my attitude, but the results are in God's hands." The tall blonde shrugged. "Easier said than done, I get that."

"Yeah, but you got the outcome you wanted."

"I did. I got far more than I wanted." Dana beamed. "I didn't just get the camp, I got Mason and Charlie, too. That'll never stop being amazing." She swept her hand around the large grand house, now bustling with life and energy even though Carson had mentioned how run-down the place had been at first. "This whole place is such a blessing. But you should know, it looks a whole lot different than how I'd planned it. I'm still working on my knack for grabbing on to my plans for myself instead of trusting them to God."

Bridget gave a sigh. "I suppose I was counting on Dad getting behind this more than I realized. Turning it into the thing that would bring him around. Maybe that's why it hurt so much when he reacted the way I should have known he would."

"Don't give up, Bridget. You're here for a few weeks. That's a lot of time for God to show up and surprise you. Trust me, He's very good at that."

Dana set her hands on her hips. "Okay, then, I'm headed out to the garden to see if…"

"Nurse Bridget!" Charlie's voice echoed from the front porch as the young boy burst through the door. "You gotta come! He's bleeding!"

Bridget ducked back into the office for her first-aid kit and cell phone as Dana called out, "Who's hurt?"

"It's Carson! He says he's okay, but he's not. Come quick!"

Carson looked up from his slow wobble across the parking lot to see Dana, Charlie and Bridget coming toward him at a panicked run.

His head was throbbing under the bloody rag he currently held to his forehead. Based on their alarmed expressions, he must look pretty bad. "I'm fine," he yelled from the distance, even though it did not feel at all fine to do so.

"I doubt that," Bridget yelled back, crossing the parking lot ahead of Dana and Charlie to grab Carson's arm. "What hit you?"

"Nothing hit me," he replied, feeling clumsy and inexpert. "I hit a low ceiling beam in the toolshed. Hard. I think I blacked out for a minute 'cause I came to on the concrete floor."

Bridget's eyes popped wide. "You lost consciousness?"

She made it sound so serious. "Maybe just got dizzy." He tried to look at her, squinting hard in the glare of the overhead sun. "Turns out you really do see stars."

She didn't appreciate the joke. In fact, she clicked into Nurse Bridget mode when he realized he was swaying against her a bit. "Grab his other arm, Dana. Let's get him inside. You hang on to us, Carson. The last thing we need is you toppling over into all this dust."

He wasn't in any condition to argue. He let Bridget and Dana guide him up the steps and through the front hall into the infirmary at the back of the house.

Through his good eye he could see Bridget grimace at his choice of triage. She probably thought the grimy rag—the only thing within reach when he'd realized just how bloody he was—did more harm than good. As if a real maintenance professional would have known better.

Bridget washed her hands and then moved to peel the thing off his forehead. Somehow, he knew it would hurt, but he also realized it probably looked even more awful than it felt. "Hey, Charlie," he said, trying to sound like all this was no big deal. "How about you and Dana go grab me one of the ice packs from the kitchen freezer?"

"On it!" the boy called as he led Dana out the door.

"Good thinking," Bridget said softly. "But that also tells me you have an idea what's under here." She pulled the rag away gently. "Yikes."

Her expression didn't do wonders for his optimism. "That's your medically professional opinion? 'Yikes'?" He tried to grin but ended up grimacing with a wince instead.

She swapped out his grimy rag with a gauze pad. Bridget's touch was gentle, her hands cool and careful. He tried not to notice how much blood was on the rag as she tossed it in the trash. "Just how big was this beam you hit? Metal or wood?"

Should he be able to answer that? "Does it matter? It was big. And hard."

Her scolding look told him. "It matters whether I need to clean out wood fragments or give you a tetanus shot. Or have Mason take you down to the medical center for stitches."

None of that sounded good. "I'm fine."

"That gets to be *my* medically professional opinion." She held his gaze. "I'm going to clean this up. It'll hurt."

He hadn't whacked his head so hard that he didn't enjoy having her so close and tending to him. "It hurts *now*," he teased.

"Hold this to your head while I get some things out. And think of something Charlie can go back to the toolshed and bring you. He should be out of the room when I do this."

That didn't inspire a lot of calm. His plan to go all tough guy and grit through whatever she had in mind suddenly felt a little shaky. Actually, all of him felt a little shaky. Maybe more than a little. Maybe he wasn't cut out for this job, after all. "I dropped my cell phone. He can go get that."

Charlie returned a second later with Dana right behind. Bridget sent the pair of them back out in search of the cell phone with a whispered, "Take a while, okay?" to Dana, who nodded in understanding.

She turned her attention back to him. "It'd be better if you can stay upright. Can you?"

"Piece of cake," he said even as he braced one arm behind him on the exam table. "Have at it."

He instantly regretted those words. Whatever she was using to clean his cut felt like gasoline. Carson gritted his teeth and dug his fingers into the exam table padding. Somewhere under all that pain he was grateful for the chance to be near her, to hear her soothing tone and see the care in her eyes.

"See if you can manage to bleed less," she joked after tossing the third darkened gauze pad into the trash.

"Yes, ma'am," he said. The roar of the sting had dulled to an ache he knew would pound for a few hours if not a few days.

Bridget leaned closer and assessed the wound. Even over the sharp scent of the antiseptic, he could smell her—her shampoo or lotion or perfume or whatever it was. It was enough to make him dizzy even without the wallop to his head.

She touched his forehead several times, a sensation as soothing to him as any bunny bandages to the youngsters. She tilted her head, her eyes narrowing as she assessed his wound. "The good news is I don't think you'll need stitches. A few butterfly bandages should do the trick. Unless you'd like a tough guy scar—stitches do a better job of that."

He didn't welcome the idea of anyone sewing up any part of him, anesthesia or not. "No, thanks. I like my face the way it is."

"Me, too," she said softly, then cleared her throat as if she hadn't meant to say that. "I'm all for scar prevention."

She hadn't quite covered the slip, and they both knew it.

The clinical tone returned to her voice as

she turned the most recent gauze pad so he could see. "I found a tiny wood fragment, so I think you're safe from a tetanus shot. I'll have Mason or somebody go out and confirm which beam you hit."

"I can do that." He should be in charge of the safety in his workshop. And no need to confirm—he was pretty sure he'd be giving that beam dirty looks for the rest of the summer.

"Oh, no. As far as I'm concerned, you're on concussion protocol for the next forty-eight hours."

"Which means...?" Some unprofessional part of him hoped concussion protocol involved constant nursing supervision. It was nice having her so close, touching him softly. Now that the pain had died down, he could almost enjoy it.

"Two days' rest, no contact sports, monitoring for headache, nausea and confusion." She reached into a drawer to produce half a dozen small rectangular packages.

He held up a hand, ticking off her list on his own fingers. "No plans for contact sports. I have a whopping headache at the moment. I feel like I'm confused half of any day. And two days' rest with monitoring would sound great if I didn't have fifty things to do right now." The last thing he wanted to do was let Mason down.

Deciding he might get away with it on a concussion-confusion excuse, he asked, "You get to monitor me, right?" Even when she shot him one of her "Nurse Bridget" looks, he couldn't quite muster up regret for the remark.

"Everyone else is as busy as you. I might need to call in Kate for reinforcements."

Chef Seb's fiancée, Kate, was a physical therapist, and as such qualified for the job, but Carson didn't want a substitute. He dared a sour look until Bridget got generous with more antiseptic. "Ouch! That stuff is nasty."

"Less nasty than an infection, I guarantee it." After a moment's thought, she pulled the headband from her hair and used it to hold back the locks of hair that covered his forehead. "Unconventional, but it'll do while I put these on."

The old Carson might find that amusing, but right now he could only imagine what his electrician friend Gordon might say if he walked in right now. "I take it these aren't Band-Aids with butterflies on them?"

She laughed. "Of course not." It had always been such fun to make her laugh. She could be so serious at times that it felt like the special gift he could give her. "Are you disappointed?"

"I'm wearing your headband. I think that's bad enough for the moment."

She began applying the bandages, and he tried not to wince or flinch when her pressure made the wound hurt. "These are supposed to be waterproof, but I never trust that. I'll have Dana find you a shower cap so you don't get these wet."

"And the indignities just keep piling up… Ow!" Before he could stop the reaction, he reached up to grab her hand as she did something that really hurt. They each froze for a moment, startled by the contact. *So she does feel it*, he thought with an inappropriate satisfaction. After all, the zing between them had never really gone away for him.

In a heartbeat, the moment was gone and she looked down to peel the next bandage from its package. "I'll go slower this time. You'll stay here in the big house with me for the next three hours, and no sleeping." She applied the next bandage with an extra gentle touch. "Can you remember the accident?"

"Vividly."

"Are you drowsy or dizzy?"

"Not anymore. Well, I was never drowsy.

But I'm not dizzy anymore." The sensation he felt having her so close was a different kind of dizzy altogether.

"We'll have someone check in on you every two hours tonight, so you should sleep here in the big house, not in your quarters."

"Okay."

She finished with the bandages and then stepped back to admire her work. Evidently finding it to her satisfaction, she gently removed the headband. "There you go, all sealed up. I expect you'll have a whopper of a headache, but no pain relievers until the first three hours have passed. You'll have to make do with the ice pack until then. And a promise to follow instructions."

If it meant getting to spend the afternoon close to her and getting such tender care, that was no chore at all. "Yes, ma'am."

She smiled. "I'm glad you're okay."

Right there was the best medicine of all. "Me, too."

Chapter Seven

Carson passed the first three hours post-injury without any complications save a long string of half-snarky, half-flirty comments Bridget was doing her best to ignore. Now, after lunch, while the camp children were in the woodshed selecting their birdhouse plans for a crafts project, there was finally a moment of quiet privacy on the porch rocking chairs.

"So, we'd like to help…if you'd be okay with that," Bridget said after she told Martina how the staff was ready to take up the idea for the bone marrow drive.

"I can't believe you'd do that. I mean, I know you—of course you're the kind of person who'd do that—but I still can't believe it. A drive? With a whole lot of people?" Martina had mentioned it offhand—more within a list of worries than a plea for help—but it had been clear to Bridget how much the need had weighed on the young mother's heart.

"You did tell me you needed a viable donor if it came to that. Why not get the largest possible pool of registrants? This could be about more than just Matteo. Don't you think many of these families would jump at the chance to save a life given the lives that have been lost to them?"

Martina looked so relieved. "I don't know what to say. I mean… I suppose some part of me thought we didn't have the right to hope. It's such a long shot."

"All the more reason for us to help. After all, wouldn't it be a massive relief to know you had access to a match?"

Martina wrapped her arms around her chest. "It's been hounding me, actually. I've been thinking I ought to start asking people—you know, go further out into the extended family, that sort of thing—but I couldn't bring myself to do it. When I mentioned it to you, I didn't…"

"I know. You weren't asking. But I tell you, Martina, the idea stuck in my head and wouldn't let go. Dana tells me that's how this whole camp got started. Why can't this be my little piece of it?"

Martina looked at her, eyes brimming. "I

don't know what to say. Other than thank you. From the bottom of my heart, thank you."

Her relief and gratitude lit a spark of excitement in Bridget's chest. "Well, I don't actually know if we can pull it off yet, but I didn't want to move forward without your okay. And even then, we both know we may not find what you're looking for. But at least we'll have tried."

Martina's shoulders softened, as if one tiny part of the enormous burden she carried had been lifted. Bridget thought of Carson's "make one thing a bit better" comment. Wouldn't it be amazing if she could make this big solution happen for the boy?

Martina wiped her eyes and looked around at the stark beauty of the land that surrounded them. "Matteo's match is here," she said with a quiet conviction. "I know it."

Bridget prayed that was true. If it was, it would be amazing. But even if it wasn't, she could pray that the whole process would be a good thing for everybody.

She was about to pull Martina into a big hug when the door from the house swung open and Seb walked out. "Your boy Carson is asking if he can take some painkillers now. The ice bags aren't cutting it. And he sure looks like he wants a nap."

Bridget rose. "I'll get him set up in the guest room on the first floor. He has to sleep here tonight, anyway. Mason, Dana and I are going to take shifts checking on him."

"Kate's off tomorrow. She said she would help, too. She could come do the dawn brigade and I'll keep Kimmy and Kent with me in the kitchen while I'm getting breakfast going." Seb's fianceé lived in a house on the edge of the camp property with her two children, and it was adorable how Seb was constantly finding ways to keep his future family close by. Kimmy and Kent were almost as much a part of the camp family as Charlie, and surely more so once the couple tied the knot at the end of the summer.

"It's so amazing how everyone pitches in here," Martina said. "Sometimes I feel so alone in Milwaukee."

Seb offered Martina a warm smile. "Pulling together is the whole point of this place."

"We're going to pull together in a really amazing way to help Matteo," Bridget replied, excited to begin spreading the word. "Martina's given the okay for us to do a bone marrow donor drive."

"Hey, that's great. I can't think of a better project for our Nurse Bridget here. Except maybe getting that cranky maintenance man out of my kitchen. I've got some killer spaghetti and meatballs to fix for Matteo tonight."

Martina's face lit up. "He told you?"

"I ask all the kids to tell me their favorites. If I can pull it off, I try to do some of the parents' favorites, too. What's yours?"

The mother's cheeks flushed. "My favorites run more along the lines of desserts."

Seb flashed an engaging grin. "I get that. Nobody said it had to be a main dish. Or even the least bit healthy. So, what is it?"

"Carrot cake," Martina replied. "With lots of cream cheese frosting."

Bridget offered a smile of her own. "I could get behind that."

Seb tapped his temple as if storing the information for later use. "Got it. I think we can make that happen."

Martina's smile made the "just a bit better" call ring loud and clear in Bridget's mind. Carson was right—the tiny details were never tiny. They added up to a journey back from all the sorrow. "One of these days we might convince Chef Seb to do a staff favorites night. After you all have had your turn, that is."

"Oh," Seb said in return, "I already know what yours is. Carson told me. Turns out the guy gets pretty talkative when you whack him on the head."

The playful look in Seb's eye grew a knot under Bridget's ribs. Carson hadn't dumped the whole dramatic story of their romantic history on Seb, had he? "What'd he say?"

"Just that a grilled cheese was the way to your heart."

The way to her heart? Did he have to use *those* words? It sounded so...so...former boyfriend. Former serious boyfriend. It was the truth, after all. It just wasn't anything she wanted everyone to know right now.

"Ohh," Martina said, sighing. "Really good grilled cheese—with thick bread and melting cheese? I agree. Delicious."

Seb ran his hands together. "Well, now, that's practically a mandate. Seriously, adult grilled cheese and carrot cake. I can make them both happen."

"This day just keeps getting better," Martina said. She gave a heartfelt look to both Bridget and Seb. "Thank you. I'm very glad to be here."

"We're glad to have you. You and Matteo both," Bridget said. "I'll get back to you with more details once I hear from the donor center, but for right now I'd better go see to my patient."

She left Martina and Seb talking about carrot cake and walked into the parlor to find Carson sprawled on the common room couch, nearly asleep. He looked scruffy with his hair sticking up in all directions above the bandages, and the makings of a spectacular shiner were blooming around his left eye. "Adorable" wasn't the right word, but his present state tugged on her heart. Mussed and half asleep, he showed too much of the lost-boy personality that had stolen her heart. Was she nostalgic for that lost boy, or blooming a new admiration for the more mature man?

No matter the answer to that question, Nurse Bridget had a job to do. She walked over and nudged Carson. When he only grumbled and didn't open his eyes, she shook his shoulder.

"Huh?" he said, still half asleep, but opened his eyes to look at her. It was a strange, unguarded moment, and she saw a stunning affection warm his eyes. He wasn't aware enough to put the careful guardrails they'd worked hard to build around their working relationship. In fact, he looked at her exactly the way he'd used to back then. The kind of look that had never failed to sweep her off her feet. "Hey," he said, reaching for her.

It took a moment to wrestle her composure back to the task at hand. "Hey there, Mr.

Todd." She felt the absurd need to use his last name, as if calling him Carson was too dangerous. "You can nap now, but you can't nap here."

He started to rise, until his head clearly reminded him why he should take it slow. "Ow."

"Easy there." She put a hand on his shoulder and guided him upright. "Sit up slowly. We're setting you up in the spare room here, remember?"

"Yeah. Sort of."

He looked a bit wobbly, so Bridget held up three fingers. "How many fingers do you see?"

That earned a drowsy scowl from Carson. "First trade school and now counting tests. Don't you people ever let up?"

What was he talking about? She wasn't going to get a sensible answer out of him now. "Just tell me how many fingers."

"Three," he grumbled and went to run a hand through his hair, then stopped himself as his fingers reached the set of bandages. "Can I go get some sleep now?"

"Do you feel steady enough? Should I go get Seb to help me get you to the spare room?" Carson was a tall, solid man. If he started to go down, Bridget wasn't sure she could catch him, and the last thing he needed to do was risk bumping that head again.

Carson stood up—slowly, thankfully—and proceeded to put his arm around Bridget. "I got all the help I need right here."

There was something remarkably familiar in his arm around her. Her body remembered the sensation instantly, before she had a chance to stop it. "Let's get you over there," she said in her best professional voice. "You'll be right across from the infirmary where I can keep an eye on you."

He smiled; a lopsided, wobbly and totally endearing grin. "I'd like that."

His head hurt. A lot of him hurt, actually. The list of things he should be doing swarmed around his head like bees. It felt like everybody wanted something from him. But he was so tired. Carson felt that despite that long list, he could sleep for a week.

He settled into the cot with a wave of gratitude, smiling up at Bridget while she fussed over him. It felt so good to have her fuss over him. He wanted to be worthy of her fussing, to be the man who deserved her care. He used to be that man, but he doubted it now. Her words and actions told him she'd only grown further out of his league. He was just a maintenance man on a camp outside town. Even if he took

Gordon up on his offer to sponsor his entry into the trade school to become an electrician, would that change anything?

Would he be good enough for her now? Ever? Her eyes told him there was still a spark of what had been between them. *I was good for her then,* he told Arthur in his mind. *You were wrong.*

"Who's wrong?" Bridget asked.

Her beautiful brown eyes came into view above him as Carson forced his lids open. "Huh?"

"You mumbled something about being wrong," she said. "Wrong about what? Are you feeling worse?"

He shook his head as much as the rattling inside would allow. "Nothing. Just mumbling." *You got her friendship back. Don't go messing it up by wanting more.*

"Okay, then. Sleep tight. I'll be right across the hall if you need me. Do you want me to shut the door?"

"No. I'll be fine." He'd once dreamed of the chance to fall asleep to the sound of Bridget's voice, and maybe this was his only chance. He couldn't think of a better way to slip into the mist.

Chapter Eight

As the days went by, Bridget felt she could declare her first week at camp a success. Bolstered, she attempted to connect with her mother and father at church services.

It did not go well.

Why had she thought the lovely sanctuary at North Springs Community Church would ease the tensions in her family? Mom and Dad—always early for church—had arrived before the collection of camp staff and families. Mason and Dana always made sure the camp families had a chance to attend church services and encouraged it at every opportunity.

It irked Bridget that Mom and Dad had placed themselves in a pew that didn't leave room for her to join them. She was ashamed of how her father's near-palpable irritation at the presence of people from Camp True North Springs distracted her from the service. *I should be here offering praise to my Heavenly Father, not grumbling about a fight with my earthly father.*

She had to find a way to work this out. The next weeks would be unbearable if she didn't. So as soon as the service ended, Bridget went straight to her parents even though she had to run to catch their quick exit. "Mom, Dad, wait!"

The clashing looks on her parents' faces startled her. Dad still looked annoyed while Mom's expression was uncomfortable and apologetic. She'd always been softer to his boldness, the caretaker to his authoritarian, but the chasm between their personalities seemed to have grown.

Mom shrugged. "We're in a bit of a hurry this morning."

Bridget doubted that—it used to take an effort to drag Mom from chatting with dozens of people at church coffee hour.

"Things to do," Dad said flatly. He scowled over Bridget's shoulder at the crowd of congregation members. He didn't need to say the presence of camp families ruined the morning for him—it showed clearly on his face.

Bridget no longer cared to dismiss his reaction. She stepped right into his field of vision, literally placing herself between her father and the families. "I don't understand this, Dad. Go meet them. They're incredible people. They're not at all what you think."

Mom's eyes silently pleaded, *Don't start.*

Her father's gaze landed on her with the weight of a boulder. "And what is it you think I think?"

Bridget gestured back toward the crowd of people pleasantly chatting with each other. "You're jumping to judgments I think are wrong. You don't know them. You haven't heard their stories. I'm sure you'd change your mind if you took the time to get to know even a few of them." She wanted to show her parents respect, but Dad was so very wrong in his viewpoint.

"I doubt that." His tone was sharp and cold. "I don't have to meet these people to know them. They've all come from trouble. They're here because they've come from trouble. From crime. We don't need that here."

"You can't treat their circumstances like crimes," she countered.

Mom seemed to worry they'd launch into a full-blown argument, and she wasn't all wrong.

Dad's jaw tightened. "I've always taught you that our choices make our circumstances. Who we choose to associate with and what we choose to allow—those things set the tone for our lives."

Where was grace in those words? Where was forgiveness? Second chances? Bridget was losing the battle to keep her composure— again—but she seemed helpless to stop her rising frustration.

"No, Dad, we *don't* always get to choose our circumstances. Sometimes things happen to us. What we *can* choose is how we react to them, how we grow from them." She rose herself up to meet her father's dark gaze. "I support Camp True North Springs. Even more than ever. Can you live with that?"

"I suppose I'll have to." He seemed to accept the strength of her stance—or at least tolerate it.

"See?" Mom cut in, eager to end things on a reconciled note. "We can work this out just fine."

Only Dad wouldn't let it go at that. "But don't you keep trying to change my mind on this. And when things go wrong—because, mark my words, they will with *those* kinds of people coming here—" he jabbed a finger at her "—don't come to me expecting to help fix it."

Mom put a hand on Dad's arm. "Arthur, please."

"'*Those* kinds of people'? What about Martina Garza? She isn't 'those kind of people.' She grew up here. And her son needs our help."

She didn't think Dad's look could get any darker. "Why are you heading that donor thing up?"

"Because it's a simple way I can help. I'm already an organ donor, this is just another way. The Busketeers are going to help us do a community drive. All the camp families are on board."

"Why must you keep bringing this up?" Dad asked. "I'm not for putting my private medical information in some database. It could end up anywhere."

There seemed little point in going over the facts again. "It could end up saving a life, Dad. That's a pretty good goal in my book. But let's be honest—this isn't about the registry. You won't help because it could help a camp family." Bridget started to walk away. "I'm disappointed, but I can't say I'm surprised."

"Well, you've made a lot of disappointing choices lately, haven't you?"

"Arthur!" Mom chided Dad's sharp tone. "I'm sorry, honey," she said to Bridget. "I think it's best we leave now."

Bridget watched them walk away. Mom and Dad didn't see eye to eye on the camp. That was clear. But there seemed to be a tension between her parents that went beyond the camp. What was it?

Carson came up beside her and offered a cup of coffee. "You okay?"

She accepted the coffee—cream and two sugars, just the way she liked it. "Dad is impossible," she groaned.

Carson sipped his own coffee. "Not really a new thing, if you ask me."

He'd been the target of Dad's judgmental nature, too. He still was. "If he'd just meet them." She sighed. "He's so convinced they're some kind of threat to North Springs." Bridget's frustration clawed at her.

Her parents' car pulled quickly out of the church parking lot. "Hard to change some people's ideas of what other people ought to be."

There was an edge to his statement, a touch of the rebellion that had been so ingrained in Carson from back then. He wasn't as settled or satisfied as he seemed to want everyone to believe. Why had he wandered so much, almost running from what she'd seen as his potential? She'd never stoop to her father's judging, but she did wonder. Did Carson see that as the same thing?

"I get that you'd like their support," Carson said after a stretch of silence, "but I don't think that's ever coming."

Mom and Dad's car disappeared up the street, a fast retreat back to their house on the hill. "Nope."

Carson took her elbow and turned her back toward the church. "So stop waiting for it, stop trying to convince them. You know the camp, and the donor drive, are the right things to do. You've got the support of a lot of other people. Church people, Busketeers, townspeople. And you've definitely got mine. So run with that. You're strong enough."

Carson's rebellious edge softened into a mischievous grin. "Plus, wouldn't it feel good to prove them wrong? I don't know about you, but I'd love to see your dad's face when the drive pulls up a match for Matteo—or anyone for that matter—and a whole lot of good comes out of this. Hard to argue with a life saved. Even the mighty Arthur Nicholson couldn't put up a fight against that."

She managed a small hopeful smile. "You don't know my dad."

He grinned right back. "Oh, yes, I do. But I also know his daughter. And I'm backing Nurse Bridget."

Carson left Bridget with her thoughts for a while as he walked back over toward the tables of coffee and cookies. He thought it clever how Chef Seb worked with the camp families each week to make batches of cookies to bring to the church's post-service coffee hour. It was an inventive and low-pressure way of making the camp families feel part of a church community while they were here. For some, it was their first experience of church, and the caring support a faith community could provide.

"It's God who does the real healing work of Camp True North Springs," Mason frequently declared. "So we do everything we can to point our families toward that truth. We don't convince them, we just nudge a bit. And sometimes that starts with cookies and coffee after a church service."

It worked both ways. The tasty partnership also allowed the townspeople to receive something from the camp families. And, from the looks of this morning's coffee hour, for conversations and relationships to begin.

This was the way around Arthur's bull-headed opposition. The long uphill battle to get the necessary zoning variance approved to turn Mason's family land into a camp was still fresh in many people's memory. Arthur made sure they didn't forget it. Carson never could understand how so many people accepted Arthur as some sort of self-appointed guardian for North Springs. Sure, he ran a successful insurance business, and chaired the zoning board and a half dozen other civic committees, but that didn't make him right. That man was on the hunt for camp failures, for even the smallest of problems the camp might bring to North Springs. If Arthur's own daughter couldn't stop him, Carson doubted the man could ever be stopped. He'd meant what he'd said to Bridget—there was no changing her father's opinion. They would simply have to go around him and succeed in spite of his disapproval.

That was a tall order for Bridget. He could see she craved a happily supportive family, the glow of her father's approval. After all, that need for Dad's approval had fueled her leaving Carson behind years before. Arthur had declared him unfit to share Bridget's future, and Bridget hadn't had the strength to stand against the condemnation. It'd hurt then. It still hurt now.

She didn't hold all her parents' judgmental nature, but there was a bit lingering under the surface. The way she asked questions about why he hadn't gone to college or what his future plans were. She had grown stronger, but she didn't seem sure that he had grown, as well. The new Bridget was bringing up a troublesome yearning in him for a second chance with her. And that was a problem, because he wasn't interested in having his heart torn apart by rejection again. He'd barely survived it the first time. A smart guy should learn from his mistakes.

Carson was still brooding over that when Gordon Jacobs walked up. *Not him right now*, Carson thought sourly. The electrician nodded at the bandages Carson still wore and the full-blown black eye he sported. "Who socked you?" Gordon was a friendly guy, and generous in his support of the camp. Still, Carson placed Gordon in the too-long line of people who seemed to think he should be doing more with his life than being the maintenance man for Camp True North Springs. Was Gordon making small talk or leading up to another conversation about trade school?

"I had a run-in with a treacherous beam in the toolshed," Carson explained for the twelfth time this morning.

"You okay?"

"I'm fine," he answered, even though he felt anything but fine. He was annoyed and frustrated and the bright sun was starting to give him a headache.

"Did Mason tell you what I said?"

So much for hope of small talk. "He did. Not really my thing, you know?"

"You'd be good. A lot of people look down their nose at the trades but there's a good living to be made."

Carson tried not to bristle. He ought to be grateful for the confidence Gordon seemed to have in him, but, in truth, it grated on his unsettled spirit. "I'm living good now."

"A single guy can get away with a lot of making do at your age. But someday you're going to want to provide for a family. Have you thought about that?"

He'd had a moment in those blurry days after the concussion. A vision of him and Bridget in a tiny house with a pair of perfectly adorable kids. Just as fast, his brain dashed the image away. Bridget wanted an upscale version of that life—one with a big house and a pair of adorably perfect children going to private schools. *Out of my league.*

"No," Carson replied more curtly than he ought to.

"Someday you'll meet a woman who will change that," Gordon replied.

"I suppose I'll just have to worry about that when the time comes."

"Well, I like to think I know talent when I see it. You know how to find me if you change your mind." Gordon offered his hand for a shake. "The offer still stands. After all, camp isn't open all year-round, you could tackle it in the winter months."

Carson shook his hand. "I'll keep that in mind."

As Gordon walked away, Carson tried not to let his words get to him. *Someday you'll meet a woman who will change that.* Bridget had been that woman, once. And look where it had gotten him—all his dreaming of a life with her fell way short against the mighty Nicholson expectations.

What if Bridget opted to stay on as the camp's permanent nurse? How she connected with and cared for the kids was impossible to ignore. Even Mason and Dana had noticed it. Bridget seemed to *belong* at the camp. She flourished there. And now she seemed strong enough to take the stand against her dad that staying there would require.

And there was the real problem if she *did* stay. Knowing she wanted nothing more than a professional relationship, could he handle being so close to her indefinitely? Could he endure just being friends with her? Did he dare admit she ran the very real danger of stealing his heart—and breaking it—all over again?

The answer made his chest ache worse than his head.

Chapter Nine

How had he forgotten how heavy stones were?

Early Monday afternoon, the first of the wall and paving stones for the memorial garden had arrived. And Carson was itching to get started. Even though Bridget had cautioned him to take things slow, he filled a wheelbarrow and began hauling stones out to the location he and Mason had chosen.

His body let him know right away it was too much too soon. It was hot, the stones were heavy, and this was challenging work. He hadn't gotten nearly far enough before he had to stop and gulp down some water.

"Need a hand?"

Carson turned to see Leo Michaels and Daniel Lohan walking toward him. Each held their own water bottles—Bridget really had

drummed into everyone to stay hydrated—
and a set of work gloves.

"Hate to admit it, but I suppose I do."

Daniel and Leo had struck up a surprising
friendship during their first week at camp, a
sort of grandpa-grandson duo that made everyone smile. "Well, then, I suppose we will,"
Daniel said.

Carson hadn't wanted to pressure any of the
families into helping with the garden. They
could contribute names to be engraved in the
pavers, or plants when the time came. But the
hard work of actual building? He was ready
to shoulder that on his own. Only it was prov-
ing harder than he'd anticipated. Maybe it was
time to admit he was glad for the help. "Much
appreciated."

Daniel looked at the wheelbarrow full of
stones. "I'll warn you, though. It might be kind
of slow help. Leo's a little guy and I'm not as
spry as I used to be."

"I'm not that little," the seven-year-old said,
making both men laugh.

"You're big enough to help in my book,"
Carson replied. "I'm supposed to be taking it
slow, anyway."

"Orders from Nurse Bridget?"

"Yep." Carson took a swig from the ever-present, Nurse-Bridget-ordered water bottles that were now everywhere at camp. "So I guess slow help's just what I need." He pointed to the curving line spray-painted onto the sandy soil. "We're lining the first row up along there. Leo, there are some smaller connector stones on the far side of the wheelbarrow. They look just about your size." Carson set down his water bottle. "If we worked together, we could have the first layer down by supper."

Daniel pulled on his gloves and nodded to the boy. "What do you say we help Mr. Carson move some stones, Leo?"

The boy nodded right back and yanked on his own smaller set of gloves. The sight made Carson want to get out his phone and take a picture to show everyone. This was the kind of connection that made the healing of Camp True North Springs happen.

Daniel passed one of the smaller connecting stones to Leo. "My Tommy used to build all kinds of things with LEGOs when he was your age." He picked up one of the larger stones with a grunt. "They were a bit lighter than these."

"I like LEGOs, too," Leo said.

Daniel bent down and lined up the stone with the markings on the soil, right next to the handful Carson had already set. For a man in his early sixties, Carson thought him more "spry" than Daniel gave himself credit for. "Like that?" Daniel asked.

"Exactly," Carson replied. "Leo, put yours right next to that last one so they make a curve." Grinning, the boy lined up his stone, giving it an adjusting tap just like Daniel had.

They worked together for a few minutes. Carson remembered Dana's advice to encourage conversations with camp families about the loved ones they'd lost. As they turned back for more stones from the wheelbarrow, he asked, "What did Tommy like to build?"

"All sorts of things," Daniel replied. "But I think he liked towers best. He was always trying to figure out how to build higher ones that wouldn't fall over. Good at it, too. It didn't surprise me at all that he wanted to become an engineer." The man paused for a thoughtful moment, running one hand over the flat surface of the stone he was holding. Carson wondered if he was picturing Tommy's name engraved on the surface. "Tommy would have built great things."

"Sure sounds like it." The families' grief was a challenge to bear, but the lost potential— the things stolen out of the world by the taking of those lives far too soon—stung sharply. That sense of loss fueled Carson's need to build, to fix, to make the camp better in any way he could.

Leo looked up to Daniel with a pride that dug deep into Carson's heart. "Tommy was a hero." Mason—who'd lost his own wife far too soon—believed this camp was one place where these families could talk about their lost loved ones and know it didn't make anyone uncomfortable. They all carried a loss and shared it freely with each other. There was a powerful healing in that.

Daniel swallowed hard as he settled the stone into place. "He was."

"He tried to keep other people safe." Leo was young for the hard story of Tommy's death, but the boy's words told Carson he already knew the tragic facts.

As the three of them built the curving wall, Carson felt safe to follow another of Dana's instructions. He asked Daniel, "Tell me more."

"Tom was out with friends at an outdoor concert. He loved music. Even played a little guitar himself. The event was over, and they were one of the last people to leave the park. A fight broke out between a couple of guys— over a girl, of course—and she ran scared toward Tom and his friends. My boy didn't hesitate to put himself between the woman and the meanest of the bunch, even when the knife came out. He stood his ground, because, well, that's who our son was."

The sorrow of the word "was" hung in the air for a moment, as heavy as the stones they were carrying.

"He saved her from that bad man," Leo said simply. How was it these kids could face up to such enormous truths like that?

Daniel put a hand on Leo's shoulder. "He did. I'll always be proud of that, even when I miss him so much."

They worked for a little while longer, each one lost in their thoughts of the tragic way Tommy had lost his life. Where was the justice in something like that? Carson hadn't lost anything and still the wrongness of it pressed down on him. How did someone like Daniel carry such a burden? How did Leo—who'd lost his firefighter father in a fire intentionally set—carry a burden like that? Suddenly the stones didn't seem that heavy.

As they got to the end of the laid-out line, Daniel wiped his brow with the back of his hand and asked, "Where's the tallest part of this wall going to be?"

Carson could almost smile, for he'd had the same thought himself. "Over there where the little entrance will be. There'll be pillars on each side with an ironwork arch between them."

"Sara and I will dedicate one of those top stones for Tommy, then. You just tell me how when all that's ready." Daniel held out a hand for a shake.

Carson knew he didn't need to clear that with anyone. Mason would certainly agree to the idea. He shook the gentleman's hand. "It'd be my pleasure, Daniel."

"I like it," Leo said, holding out his own hand to shake each of the men's. " Do you think my dad could have the one on the other side?"

"I can't think of anything I'd like to see more," Carson said. "I'm sure we can make that happen. And I expect I'll always think of the arch between them as Leo and Daniel's arch, because you connect the two." A bit poetic—more the way Bridget might have seen it—but true nonetheless. The three of them stood there for a minute, picturing what the finished wall and arch would look like. Like the welcome burst of a breeze that came through just then, the power of the moment swept over all of them.

"Well," Daniel said as he cleared his throat, "we got a lot more stones to move before we get that far. Best keep at it."

If there was an unofficial motto of Camp True North Springs, that might have been it. Best Keep At It And Make It Just A Tiny Bit Better.

Carson knocked on Bridget's door an hour after supper Tuesday while the families were all gathering with Dana and Mason around the evening campfire. He looked rough around the edges, eyes squinting and moving with the ungraceful gait of a man whose body hurt more than he'd planned.

She'd seen another delivery of the stones and then caught sight of him up on the part of the property where the memorial garden would be. It wasn't hard to guess the source of his pain. Bridget set down the book she'd been reading and gave him a bit of a scowl. "I distinctly remember telling you to take it easy. Those stones could have waited for a cooler day."

"I ran out of patience." Carson flexed his shoulders and pinched the bridge of his nose. "Now I'm hoping you haven't run out of Tylenol and ice."

Bridget rose from the chair and unlocked the

medicine cabinet. "A good nurse never runs out."

"Good thing you're a good nurse."

She pulled the bottle of pain medicine from the shelf. "When's the last dose you took?"

"Just after lunch. It's worn off."

Bridget checked her watch. "I expect it has. Did you eat dinner?" She hadn't seen him around the dining hall's big tables.

"I sort of fell asleep after hauling all those stones. Slept through it."

She pocketed the bottle and began walking toward the kitchen. "Well, that's not helping things. Let's get some food in you, too."

He stopped, brightening. "Maybe a grilled cheese?"

"I was thinking more like some of Seb's leftover lasagna."

"But you make the best grilled cheese." His words had a pouty tone worthy of Leo. "Or you used to. Did all that fancy ship food knock that out of you?"

He was teasing her, and she shouldn't rise to his bait, but the man had a talent for making apologetic discomfort charming. Scruffy, stubborn and just the right amount of needy. "I still make a fabulous grilled cheese," she declared, even though it had been ages since she'd made one.

"I feel like it's a necessary element of my recovery."

Bridget gave him a sideways glance as they made their way toward the kitchen. "Grilled cheese sandwiches do not have medicinal properties."

Carson gave her a look that definitely belonged on Leo more than a man of his nearly thirty years. "Says you."

She decided to use this moment to negotiate. "How about this? I will make you a grilled cheese *if* you ice your head while I'm doing it *and* promise me not to work four hours out in the hot sun hauling stones tomorrow."

"You were counting?"

Bridget filled a water glass and reached into the freezer for an ice pack. "Daniel came up to me at dinner and told me to keep an eye on you, that he thought you might be overexerting yourself again today."

"The old man ratted me out?"

"And Leo. Seems you made quite an impression on them both."

Carson held the pack to his head and sighed with relief. "At first, I wasn't sure they should help—I mean they're guests, not staff. But it turned out to be really meaningful. For all of us. Yesterday, Daniel told me about how his son Tommy was killed. Heartbreaking stuff. But Dana's right, it is important for them to be able to talk about it."

Bridget handed Carson the pain tablets. "I read the file. That's a difficult story to tell in front of someone as young as Leo."

"You'd think." Carson swallowed the pills and sat down while Bridget began rifling through the cabinets and fridge for a frying pan and ingredients. "Only Leo could see the heroism beyond the tragedy. Even at his age. Does that make any sense?"

"Leo's father was his own kind of hero— a firefighter. With his life taken too soon just like Tom Lohan. So yeah, it makes a kind of sense."

"You should see how those two connect. It's amazing. Everything about what this place is wrapped up in, two people you'd never expect to be friends." Carson shifted the ice pack. "Do you ever…feel like we don't deserve to be here? I mean everyone here has suffered such a huge loss. We've had things happen to us—I don't mean to say that breaking off your engagement wasn't a big thing—but…" His words fell off and he shrugged as if he couldn't figure out how to say what he wanted to convey.

And there it was; the passion for the mission of this camp that shone so brightly in his eyes. It radiated off him, tired and hurting as he was. Carson could always catch the vision of something and put his whole heart into it. She'd loved that about him. Anders was important, but it was as if he'd merely added her into his circle of influence. That wasn't the same thing. When she had been with Carson, back when they were together, he'd made her feel like the most important thing in the world. She hadn't realized the difference until just this moment, and it pulled at her in ways she wasn't quite ready to admit.

Still, she reached out and touched his arm. "You belong here. You're exactly what this place needs."

"This place needs more than me. It needs an electrician and a plumber and half a dozen other skills I don't have."

"Skill can be learned. You just have to want to learn them. You could be what Mason and Dana need." The words felt like a throwback to their past, suddenly making it hard to keep that line she'd drawn back on her first day.

He held her gaze, strong and steady, making Bridget worried he'd say something about her being what he needed. That wasn't a safe place to go. "You belong here, too," he said, his tone too warm. "You're different than when you arrived. Even stronger than the Bridget I knew." He paused for a moment. "Have they asked you about staying?"

She was not at all ready to admit the thought had crossed her mind. She knew this place had changed her. The broken engagement no longer loomed as a catastrophe—it never had been, really. More like a long-overdue course correction, to put it in nautical terms. But that didn't mean Camp True North Springs was where her course should take her now. There were far too many complications to begin thinking like that.

"No."

"But you've thought about it?" Carson pressed, sensing the questioning in her tone. He'd always been too good at reading her.

She busied herself with the tasks of cooking. "It's fine for now. Just until I figure out what comes next." The sizzle of the buttered bread hitting the skillet filled the room. She'd forgotten how good a grilled cheese in the making smelled. She knew Carson was watching her, but she didn't look up for fear of how those eyes would pull down her defenses.

"You know your dad is wrong, don't you?"

"About the camp?" she managed, aware of what he might really be asking. "About the donor drive?"

Carson kept silent, and she knew his gaze was still fixed on her. She knew his silence was a challenge; that he was waiting for her to say she regretted how things had ended between them. She did regret *how* they'd broken things off, but she wasn't quite ready to say it was wrong *that* they'd broken it off. That idea was far too dangerous to ponder at the moment. Just because her feelings for him were resurfacing at an alarming rate didn't mean their lives were headed in compatible directions. She needed to be careful how she charted her course from here.

"Yes, Dad is wrong about lots of things."

It wasn't the answer he wanted. But it was the only answer she could give right now.

Chapter Ten

Bridget stood in the church driveway Thursday morning with Dana and several other women from North Springs, including her mom, Hannah from the grocery store, Rita Salinas and Marion Gilbert.

"Are you sure, Marion?" Pastor Gorman asked. "Really sure?"

The question was certainly called for, given that each of the women stood over a table filled with china plates and saucers from Marion's home. And they were all holding hammers.

"You can *buy* tiles for mosaics, Marion," Rita said. "We don't have to get them this way."

Almost everyone in town knew the massive collection of china figurines and such in Marion's home. Kids called her the "China Shop Lady" even though few children dared to venture into the castle of breakable things that was Marion's house just off the town square. Dana had rented the place for a while when she'd first come to North Springs and spoke of the home as a minefield of fragile decor. Everyone seemed astounded that Marion had offered up this collection of china to break apart for a camp mosaic art project.

"Yes, we do. I have too much of this stuff. We all know that. I have to start getting rid of it before something happens and my son has to do it." Marion looked understandably anxious given what was about to happen.

"But there are less drastic ways to do that," Mom said. "Isn't this a bit…extreme? No one thinks anything is going to happen to you."

Marion squared her shoulders and put on the safety goggles Carson had sent down the mountain with Bridget and Dana. "Something's going to happen to all of us one day. And yes, this is extreme. I need extreme. Put those glasses on, ladies, we're going to break things."

Mom looked at Bridget as if this was the oddest church gathering she'd seen in ages. She had to agree.

"You heard the lady," Pastor Gorman said with equal parts humor and worry. He stepped back and gestured toward the head of the table. "But, Marion, I think it's only fitting you take the first whack."

Rita Salinas raised her hammer as if it was a salute to Marion's determination, and all the women did the same. "Lead the way," Rita said with eyes that sparkled behind her safety goggles, "and we'll all follow."

If change had a sound, it was the clear, sharp crack of Marion's hammer as it split a blue china candy dish in two. It startled everyone around the table for a second, but the expression of release on Marion's face soon brought hammers down on each of the dishes sitting in front of the collection of women. Bridget thought she'd never find the words to explain the odd experience. She knew Marion only by the older woman's near-hoarder reputation, but it was as if years fell off her with each cracked plate. There was even some laughing and a few yelps as the stack of brightly colored circles transformed into a rainbow of small pieces.

Bridget looked at the pile and imagined the brightly colored frames that would eventually grace the number markers on each guest room door at the camp. And a few ornaments for the flower and vegetable greenhouse as well as the memorial garden.

"These will make such beautiful things for the camp," Dana said, echoing Bridget's thoughts. "And I love that they came from you." After a small pause, she asked Marion, "Do you regret it at all? They were so pretty."

"They're still pretty," Marion said with a confidence that seemed to surprise the gathered ladies. "And now they're useful, too." She gave a little laugh that was almost a girlish giggle, turning to hug Dana. "I hadn't expected it to feel this good."

"Well, we've got all we need, if not a bit more," Dana declared. "I think we can safely say we're done for now. I can't wait to show you the finished frames. You'll be part of camp for a long time to come."

The group broke out into happy applause, then began lifting the pieces into plastic containers and sweeping away the dust—but not before Dana took a photo of the smashing crew with their hammers and safety goggles.

Bridget's grin lingered as she walked with her mother to the church parking lot. The tension finally began to ease between the two of them. Seizing the moment, she motioned for her mother to sit down on the set of benches tucked under the shade of the large tree in the church's side yard. "I was surprised to see you here."

"Oh, I wouldn't have missed it. We all know Marion and her house. Camp or no camp, this was history in the making."

That opened the door to the question she really wanted to ask. "Is that why Dad was okay with you coming here?"

Mom gave a long exhale. "Your father was not pleased I came this morning." She looked at Bridget. "But being married doesn't mean you have to agree on everything. Just the big things."

"Dad definitely sees the camp as a big thing." She dared to ask her mother, "Do you agree?"

Mom took a long time to answer. "I think your father's concerns aren't…unfounded. We've had a lot of struggles with people from the rehab center. We're not that big a town. He just thinks there's only so much we can shoulder without paying a price. How do we say no to the next charity? When is it too much?"

It seemed an oddly transactional way to view Camp True North Springs' purpose. Grace and hope and mercy weren't things that could be plotted on a table of risks and benefits. Most of what happened up the mountain defied logic.

It's what made the whole mission so compelling. "Do you really think of it that way?"

"I worry," Mom admitted. "I worry for you. There are so many sad stories up there, and you've come through such a difficult time. We were so happy for you and Anders. You had such a bright future ahead of you."

"No, Mom, we didn't. It looked like it at first, but I wouldn't have been happy. His family wasn't…" She searched for the kindest words to describe the disapproval she'd felt from Anders's family, knowing full well any words she used could have also been used to describe how Dad had viewed Carson.

Carson's *Your dad is wrong about a lot of things* echoed in the back of her mind and tightened her throat. Had she been wrong to let him convince her to break things off with Carson? She didn't trust the doubts swirling around her mind lately. It took more than attraction—more than love, even—to make a lifetime work with someone. "It wouldn't have worked with Anders. The truth is I broke it off before it fell apart on its own."

Mom reached over and took Bridget's hand. "Are you sure?"

"Yes." She gave her mother's hand a squeeze. "We didn't agree on the big things. It was just hard to see that on the *Brilliance*. And we couldn't stay on that ship forever."

Mom seemed to take a moment to gather courage before asking, "Do you really have to be so involved up there?"

Even though she had an idea, Bridget asked, "What do you mean?"

"Living up there. Going beyond nursing duties. Getting so invested in the people. That sort of thing."

Bridget wasn't sure if Mom was referring to the bone marrow donor drive or Carson. She chose the safer of the two subjects. "I'm happy to help with the drive. It was my idea—well, my idea to act on the problem when Martina mentioned it."

Her mother turned to face her squarely. "Don't get involved with her, Bridget. You weren't friends before, why start now? People like that never stop needing."

Mom's attitude bothered Bridget. "She's a young widow with a son facing a serious illness. I know we weren't good friends when we were younger, but I like her. I like Matteo. Why wouldn't I do something to help when I can?"

Mom shook her head. "Because it won't stop there. There'll always be something she needs from you. Tragedy follows people like that.

Don't you think it's odd she came all the way from Milwaukee after being away from North Springs for so long?"

This condemnation was starting to sound an awful lot like Dad's view. He felt that what had happened to Martina—or any of them—was somehow their own fault. "People have come to the camp from all over the country, Mom. And her parents live in Scottsdale. And, really, why does any of that matter?"

"I just don't want her using you. You have a good heart with a lot to give, you're in a tender place, and I don't want anyone taking advantage of that. Not Martina, and certainly not Carson."

"Mom, Carson and I are fine. We're past that." Even as Bridget said the words, they had a hint of falsehood. She was feeling drawn to him, to many things about who he was now, but there were still parts of him that told her she had no business encouraging anything beyond friendship.

Mom knew her well enough to catch the slight doubt in her tone. "Are you?"

Bridget stood up. "No one's taking advantage of me. Not Martina, not Carson. I like what I'm doing up there. It feels good. Like I'm making a difference—which is exactly what I *need* to feel like right now. I don't understand why you and Dad can't see that. Why you don't show any confidence in me."

Mom rose. "We're worried about you. You're vulnerable right now."

"You keep saying that. As if I need to be protected. I can protect myself. So if you're asking why I'm living up there, getting 'invested' as you say, it's because they're invested in me. They're confident in me. And there doesn't seem to be much of that coming from you and Dad." Bridget finally let the earlier words come to the surface. "He's wrong. About a lot of things."

As she headed for her car, Bridget didn't turn back around, even when her mother called, "Not about everything."

About everything that matters, Bridget thought with a stab to her heart. *All the big things.*

Carson heard the little boy's whimpers long before Rob Jennings walked into the workshop Friday afternoon. He didn't get a lot of visitors, much less ones with tears in their eyes. Rob sadly clutched a truck to his chest while his older brother, John, looked at a loss.

Carson crouched down to Rob's level. "Hey there. Why the long face?"

John nodded to his little brother. "His truck broke." Carson could tell the older boy found his brother's tears a bit much.

With a glimpse at the recently bandaged skinned knee, Carson worked out what had happened. "You and your truck took a tumble, huh?"

"He rolled off the front porch steps," John said. "Well, both of them did."

"Ouch." Carson peered into Rob's wide, wet eyes. "You okay?"

"I hurt my knee."

"Looks like you already saw Nurse Bridget to take care of that. Smart move. A superhero Band-Aid goes a long way in the healing department if you ask me."

"She said maybe you can fix the truck," John said. "It's his favorite."

Carson offered them both a smile. "I've got a favorite truck myself. Only mine's a bit bigger. But I'd be sad if it broke, too." He held out his hand for the truck. "Can I take a look?"

Rob offered the dented toy with a cautious care that let Carson know this was serious business. He needed to find a way to fix Rob's truck. He turned the red metal truck this way and that, discovering a dent and a stuck wheel.

As he made his inspection, Bridget appeared

in the shop doorway. "See, Rob, I told you Mr. Carson would help."

"Of course, I will."

Rob looked enormously relieved, as did John.

Carson walked over to the workbench and pulled up two metal stools. "Wanna hop up here and watch me work? You can even help if you like." Out of the corner of his eye, he caught a smile on Bridget's face. He'd seen her work, now he got the chance to let her watch him. The satisfaction of that sent a small glow under his skin. "What we got here is a classic case of misalignment."

Rob's eyebrows arched at the long word. "Huh?"

"Your wheel's out of whack," John said with a know-it-all tone.

Big brothers are all the same, Carson thought to himself, remembering a few condescending remarks from his own older sibling.

"But we can fix that wheel," Carson announced. "The dent might be a bit harder."

"Every tough guy needs a scar," Bridget offered as she walked up to the worktable.

Carson caught on to Bridget's tactic and ran with it. "Well, sure. This is a tough truck. Strong. Been through a lot, I'd guess." He looked at the boys. "You guys, too. Got any scars?"

With the pride any small boy would have, Rob hoisted an elbow and pointed to a patch of lighter skin. "Yep. From when I fell on my scooter last summer."

"John?"

John didn't look so keen to play the game. But with a look from his brother, he lifted his hair to show a scar running across his hairline. "Skateboard."

"What do you know? Me, too." Carson pulled back a section of hair to show a different scar than the wound still healing from the recent encounter with the toolshed beam.

"I remember when you got that." Bridget's low laugh colored the tone of her words. "The curb on the far side of the park, right?"

Rob looked intrigued. "What were you doing? Were you skateboarding, too?"

Carson tamped down his own laugh. He'd been showing off a backflip from his high school gymnastics days in an attempt to impress Bridget. There had been a lot of humiliation when he'd missed the landing, and a lot of blood. Not the kind of thing a grown man should admit to a set of impressionable boys.

"Mr. Carson was trying to impress me with something he used to be able to do in high school."

This brought a shocked look to John's face. "You two knew each other in high school?"

There was far too much history behind the answer to that. Carson stuck to the facts. "We both grew up in North Springs." They hadn't had much to do with each other in high school. He'd noticed her—how could you *not* notice her?—but he'd always considered Bridget Nicholson out of his league. He'd always considered it one of the great wins of his life when Bridget had begun to notice him one summer when she was home from nursing school. It had made him feel like the king of the world to catch her heart, to think someone from the outskirts of North Springs could land a girl from one of the town's leading families. A blessing he could scarcely believe he'd deserved. And how right that had turned out to be in Arthur Nicholson's point of view.

"Mr. Carson was on the gymnastics team, and he could do a backflip. *Back then*," she added with a humbling emphasis. "Not the time he tried to show off for me in the park."

John evidently found this impressive. "You can do a backflip?"

"I think the point is that I *could* do a backflip *once*, but not anymore. Certainly not when I gave myself this," he added, pointing to the scar.

"We flipped off the steps," Rob said. "The truck and me both."

"It was pretty funny, if you ask me," John remarked, earning a frown from Bridget.

"And you fared better than me, kid," Carson replied. "Looks like you only needed a Band-Aid. I needed sixteen stitches." *But it was worth it*, his memory added. Bridget had nursed him, even then. When she'd kissed his cheek, he'd been dizzy from far more than the collision with the concrete.

"But my truck?"

Carson returned his focus to the task at hand. "I'll have to take the wheel off. But don't worry, I'll put it back on again. I can hammer most of this dent out, but it won't look like the other side. It'll be a tough guy scar. Well, tough *truck* scar."

Rob thought about this for a moment. "That's okay. Will it still work?"

Pliers in hand, Carson began to work the toy wheel off its axle. "Good as new."

"Mr. Carson is very good at his job," Bridget said.

Carson enjoyed the praise. "So is Nurse Bridget. She fixed me up when I whacked my head earlier, remember?"

Rob pointed to the remnants of Carson's

black eye. "Yeah. You looked funny with your head all wrapped up."

Nodding toward the toolshed, Carson glowered. "I'm still holding a grudge." He peered down at the truck, finding the axle bent as well as the wheel. It was going to take a bit of tweaking to put little Rob's truck to rights. "This might take a while. Can I keep your truck until dinner?"

John gave an unsympathetic moan when Rob looked worried at the prospect of being away from his prized toy for that long.

Bridget leaned in. "Why don't you two head back into the big house and see if Chef Seb needs help setting out the afternoon snacks? Rumor is he has brownies today."

That did the trick. Both boys hopped off the stools and dashed toward the workshop door. "I'll come find you the minute it's fixed," Carson called.

"Poor Doug." Bridget sighed as the boys tumbled out of sight. "That dad is doing a great job, but three kids on your own is a handful." She met Carson's eyes with a smile. "You were sweet with them."

Carson attempted a casual shrug. "They're cute kids. And I understand a man's love for his truck."

That made her laugh. He liked making Bridget laugh. She used to do a lot of laughing, but not so much in her time here. The urge to fix that called even more powerfully than the compulsion to play mechanic with Rob's dented truck. He wanted to fix a lot of things for her, but she was still holding him at arm's length. Could he change that? Should he even try?

She gave a little knowing hum, as if she was remembering something pleasant. "You always did love your truck."

Carson vividly remembered the nights they'd sat in the bed of his rusty old pickup, staring up at the stars and making wild plans for their future. Did she? "Much better truck now," he said, tilting his head in the direction of the fancy pickup he now drove. "Better man now, too, I hope," he ventured, just to see what she would say to that.

"Seems that way to me." A hint of affection flickered in her eyes for a moment. A tiny spark of admission that the flame between them hadn't entirely burned out.

And then she turned to go, cutting the moment short. He felt her exit as an almost physical sensation, like the sun pulling the warmth from the air as it set.

Chapter Eleven

Monday morning, Carson caught up with Bridget as she was helping Martina load Matteo into the back seat of her car. The boy hadn't seemed to be doing well over the weekend, and Bridget reported growing concern at the daily staff meetings. It was time to take Matteo to get checked out at the medical center in town.

Bridget loaded a bag into Martina's trunk. "Keep me posted, and let them know they can send any instructions or treatments here to me."

"You need two bags for a checkup?" Carson asked as he picked up the second bag and tucked it in Martina's trunk.

"It's not always just an appointment, even when you think it is." Concern drew Martina's features tight. "We always pack for three days, no matter what. Things can turn on a dime like that." She snapped her fingers on the final word.

Bridget gave Martina a hug. "We'll be saying prayers for this just to be a minor bump in the road. You won't miss Chef Seb's delicious roast chicken tonight."

"You say those prayers," Martina pleaded. "I hope I see you soon."

Carson didn't see a lot of hope in Martina's eyes. Nobody wanted Matteo's visit to Camp True North Springs to be cut short by anything, least of all a medical complication. He stood beside Bridget and waved with as much optimism as he could muster as Martina drove down the driveway and through the camp gates.

"What's up?" he asked Bridget as they watched the dust cloud recede down the mountain road.

"Matteo's been running a low-grade fever. The little guy's been trying to hide that he doesn't feel well, only Martina realized he was having night sweats."

"It's Arizona in the summer. Doesn't everybody sweat day and night here?"

Bridget shot him a dark look. "Low-grade fever and night sweats are bad signs for Matteo. She's taking him down to the medical center for some bloodwork. It could be just a run-of-the-mill bug..."

"Or the cancer coming back?" Carson felt a stab to his chest at the mere idea. That little guy facing another round of cancer felt like the unfairest of unfair things. The fear in Martina's eyes would stick with him for a long time. So would the deep concern and heartbreak in Bridget's. He was almost afraid to ask, "What do they do then?"

"More chemo. But Martina thinks that will definitely mean they'll need to consider a bone marrow transplant. She pulled me aside and asked me to do whatever I could to help her find a donor, Carson." She swallowed hard, fighting back the compassionate tears he could see gathering in her eyes. "What if we can't?"

He took her by the shoulders. "What if we *can*? Come on, you've heard the stories Dana and Mason tell. God shows up in big ways on this mountain. We just need to fire up those Busketeers and get the registration going." This was Bridget's project, but he felt the "we" he'd used in his words down to his bones. "If Matteo's under any kind of threat, you know everyone here will do anything they can. So tell me, what's first?" If he could get Bridget into action mode, she'd move like a force of nature.

She turned to look back at the road. "We wait for the bloodwork to come back."

Sitting and waiting weren't Bridget's strengths. "Do we have to? I mean, the donor drive is worthwhile no matter if Matteo needs it right now, or six months from now, or never. If it's not to treat him, it could save other people. So how do we kick it into gear now?"

He was grateful to see the gears begin to turn in her head. "I've got an appointment to talk to the registry tomorrow. Then I think we just pick a date for them to bring the technicians or send the kits out. We get people to show up and start swabbing."

Carson pointed to the big house where her office was. "So get it started. The Busketeers said they needed a Saturday for the pancake breakfast, right? We've got one more Saturday in this camp session."

"We've got just enough time to make this work." The determination came back into Bridget's eyes and her tone.

"And here I thought maybe I'd get my project done before yours," he teased.

"You're still supposed to be taking it slow, remember." There was just enough humor in her voice to let him know she'd come back from the edge of her despair.

"Me, yeah. But not you. You can go full speed ahead." He thought he ought to say it. "If you're ready to defy your dad, that is." Kicking the bone marrow donor drive into high gear would drive the wedge between Bridget and her father even deeper. She likely knew that, but he wanted to make sure she launched this battle with her eyes wide open. Or at least as open as her heart.

The fire behind her eyes told him long before her nod. "Oh, I'm ready."

"Go get 'em, B."

It was what he'd called her back when they were together. When she'd gotten an idea in her head and went at it with all her heart, he'd called her a buzzing B because she'd practically vibrated with determination. He hadn't dared to use the pun nickname until just now. Partly because it harkened back to what they'd been to each other, and partly because he'd not seen "B" show up until now.

She smiled, catching the reference. It was a sweet, nostalgic smile, much different than the "keep this strictly friendly" speech she'd given him back on that first day.

She nodded and turned toward the big

house. As she walked away from him, Carson realized he was coming to care for her. The huge risk of rejection still loomed. He had no more improved credentials than the ones she'd walked away from years earlier. She was still out of his league. Trouble was, his heart wasn't interested in respecting any of that, nor the line she'd drawn between them.

He was just wrestling that ache into some kind of control when Bridget turned around, dashed back to him and gave him a hug. The sensation of her hands tight against his back and her cheek resting even briefly against his chest nearly destroyed his resistance. The two seconds she stayed in his arms felt like half a lifetime.

She had to have felt it, too. An avalanche could have swept through the camp and it wouldn't have struck this hard. When she gave his cheek a quick peck and then pulled away as if it jolted her as much as it sent a jolt through him, he knew she *did* feel it.

"Thanks," she said, breathless and flushed.

He fought the urge to keep her there in his arms, to hold on to that bliss for just a few more seconds. "Yeah," he mumbled out. "Sure, anytime. He's gonna be okay," he managed to say, desperate to find something ordinary to pull him back from the wild sensations banging around his chest. "It's all gonna be okay."

But was it? Things were either falling into place beyond anything he dared to hope, or they were about to fall apart on a monumental scale.

Only God knew which.

Bridget felt her heart twist as she took a phone update from Martina three hours later. "They want to keep him overnight. Run more tests. See if they can get the fever to go away."

"Good thing you packed for it." Bridget tried to sound encouraging. "I would have run things down for you if you needed."

"Thanks," came the weary reply, "but we're used to this."

How could anyone grow used to something like that? Disappointment pressed down on Bridget's shoulders. She'd prayed so hard that the mother and son would come back with an all clear for Matteo, as had all the staff and many of the families. That prayer hadn't been answered—yet. "We'll keep on praying for you."

Bridget heard a door shut. "They talked about it," Martina said in a whisper Bridget guessed was designed to stay out of Matteo's hearing. "Even if the bloodwork doesn't come back with...issues."

Bridget didn't have to ask what "it" was. "I've put in a call to meet with the registry people tomorrow, Martina. The Busketeers and everyone are just waiting for the word. We're going to give Matteo and anyone else the best shot we can."

"Thank you." The words were thick with a mother's concern.

"How fast... If they end up needing to... How much time do you have?"

Martina sniffed. "I don't know. Matteo needs to be in remission for them to do the transplant. They can't do anything until they actually find a match. There's an option they can do with Matteo's own cells if needed, but it doesn't work like a transplant of healthy cells. It's so scary, I can't really understand it. I don't want us to have to go there. What we need is a match."

"Keep the faith," Bridget pleaded. "You said yourself you thought there was a match for him here. Maybe that's God's way of letting you know there's reason to hope. By the time you get back, we'll probably have the whole thing set up. And, Martina, I'm going to be the first in line to donate." Bridget hadn't decided that until just this minute, but it seemed like the best way to put her commitment to the project into action.

There was a pause on the line and Bridget imagined Martina being overcome with gratitude. This must be such a scary time for her, fearing the worst for her son after so much sadness had already visited her life. "You okay?" she asked gently.

"Have you told your dad you're doing this?"

Bridget had tried not to mention her father's obstinate disapproval of the camp and the donor drive, but it had crept its way into the conversation at least once. "Don't you worry about Dad. Or anyone else who might put up a fuss. You've got loads of people ready to support you."

"I hope you can bring him around."

That's how big Martina's heart was—she was concerned for Bridget's family conflict in the middle of her own crisis. "Like I said, it won't matter. I hope he does, and I'll try one more time over the weekend, but I'm ready if he doesn't."

"Okay. Thank everyone for me and I hope I see you soon. I've got to get back to Matteo."

"Tell him he's in our prayers and we can't wait to see him back at camp."

As she hung up the phone, Bridget paused for a moment at the solid sense of conviction that settled in her. She was ready to go through with this with or without her parent's support. The shadow of her father's control had loomed over her for too long—longer and darker than she'd realized. This was about so much more than giving Matteo a shot at a healthy future should he need it. This wasn't even about defying her father's opinion. This was about following her own path in life, the one God was laying out before her.

And that path led up this mountain, to this place. Maybe not just temporarily. She couldn't deny the sense of belonging that had filled her from her first days at Camp True North Springs. This wasn't at all where she'd seen her future a month ago. Still, part of her was coming to believe this might be where her future lay.

One thing was certain—if her future was here, she was going to need to get her parents to make peace with that. Or at least try. And maybe keep trying for as long as it took. She hoped the first step might be this donor drive. If she could get Dad to let go of his opposition to this, then someday he might lay down his opposition to the camp itself.

Picking up her cell phone, Bridget called her father's office number. She almost hung up when his voicemail kicked in but decided obstacles—even small ones—would not stop her.

"Hey, Dad. I'm headed into town tomorrow and I'm going to stop by your office. I want to talk to you about something." The old Bridget might have formed it like a question, but she wasn't going to be that kind of daughter anymore.

She gathered her files for the meeting with the registry representative and looked around the camp until she found Dana and Mason with Carson and all the guests in the greenhouse.

She pulled Mason aside. "I spoke to Martina. They're staying overnight to run some tests."

Mason frowned. "That doesn't sound promising."

"She sounds worried. She said they talked to her about the bone marrow transplant again."

Dana stood up and walked over to Bridget and Mason. "That makes things more serious for him, doesn't it?"

"Yes, but there's still a chance he won't need it. It does sound like it's closer to happening. I'm glad we're doing the drive either way. Matteo needs us."

Mason shifted his weight. "It's still a long shot. Remember what Martina said—matches outside of families are rare."

Carson joined the conversation. "Rare still means possible. And there's no downside to us helping. Even if Matteo doesn't find a match, or doesn't even need a transplant, there might be someone else we can help. Who here wouldn't jump at the chance to save a life?"

Carson's support warmed Bridget's heart and fed her determination to make this happen. She was glad he'd come back into her life. She just needed to keep the proper guardrails around her feelings for lots of reasons. "I'm heading down to Phoenix tomorrow to meet with the person from the registry. And..." Bridget hesitated for a moment, knowing the reception she might get for her next announcement. "I'm going to try talking to Dad one more time."

Carson's eyes filled with doubt.

Dana gave Bridget a worried look. "Are you sure you want to do that?"

Bridget met Carson's gaze, then Dana's. "Yes. I'm sure. I don't need his support. I'm planning to move forward without it. But part of me is hoping he'll come around to respecting—maybe someday supporting—what I decide to do. We're going to have to learn how to disagree, him and me." If she ever did decide to stay here permanently, she'd need to find a way for it not to fray her family ties. She borrowed one of Dana's favorite phrases. "But God's going to have to show up in a big way to make that happen."

Chapter Twelve

Dad glared at her from behind his enormous desk Tuesday morning. "Why are we going over this again? You know my position."

Bridget straightened. "Because your position is wrong."

"You're young. You've always been idealistic. It's time to grow up and see how the world really works."

His dismissive tone dug under her skin. "You mean how *you* think it works. You're convinced the camp will damage North Springs, but I believe the camp is a good thing for us. A chance to show community and support. To be all the things people of faith are supposed to be." *Instead of judgmental*, she added silently in her mind.

"We are all those things without that camp.

We don't need those people and their problems. It's enough of a fight to keep the land around here private property. If everyone tossed the rules out like Mason did, who knows what we'd end up with?"

Why did I come here thinking things would be any different? Bridget struggled to keep the conversation civil and respectful. "I'm sorry we disagree so strongly on this."

Her quieter tone diffused some of Dad's anger. "I just don't understand why you feel compelled to go up there and help them. I know things have fallen apart for you, but this isn't the way to deal with that."

No matter how she explained it, Dad still saw the broken engagement as something that had happened to her, not a choice she'd made. Or, at the very least, a poor choice she'd made. Could she ever make him understand how breaking things off with Anders had been the right decision? How she was coming to believe that going up there to help Camp True North Springs was a good path for her? "I'm not sure I can explain it to you, Dad. Only that I don't regret breaking up with Anders. Can you accept that?"

"You're asking me be fine with how my

daughter seems to be throwing her future away."

Her father could so easily boil up anger in her. "I'm asking you to accept my choice. I'd rather you supported it, but I'll take your tolerance if that's all I can get."

Dad shook his head. "This will all be over after the weekend anyway, and you can get on with your real future. I called the head of the nursing staff down at Sun Valley Health Systems the other day, and he said they'd be happy to interview you."

Bridget felt her jaw drop. "You called someone to get an interview for me? Dad, I'm almost twenty-eight. Do you have any idea how that looks?"

"One of their board members is a client of mine. It looks like a father using his connections on behalf of his daughter," he replied.

She stood up and paced the large office. "No. That's not how it looks. It completely undermines my professionalism." She turned to give him a glare of her own. "I don't need my father job-hunting for me."

"Well, you need *someone* nudging you in the right direction," he shot back. "You're certainly not going to get it up on that mountain."

Nothing could be further from the truth. She

felt a stronger sense of direction—a glimpse of her own true north—up on that mountain than she had felt in years. "I came here hoping I could get even a bit of support from you. If not for the camp, then for the donor project I'm heading up for Matteo Garza. So many other people are ready to rally around that little guy to sign up to be a bone marrow donor. I'm heading down to Phoenix to set up the date now. And if you think that doesn't make our town better, then I don't know what we have to say to each other." She grabbed her handbag and her files, filled with disappointment and anger.

As she reached the door, Bridget added, "As a matter of fact, I'm taking the test and registering today, if they let me. I think Matteo and Martina are worth my help, even if you don't."

Dad rose out of this chair to plant his hands on his desk. "I forbid it."

"You what?"

"I said I forbid you to take that test."

Bridget stared at him, unable to believe what he'd said. "You can't forbid me. I'm a grown woman. I don't need your approval to do anything. Or have you never realized that?"

"Don't you dare help those people like that. It's not just like writing a check, Bridget. It's a part of your body. Who knows what could happen?"

"I could save a little boy's life, that's what could happen. Or someone else's. What have you got against the Garzas, anyway? Or is it just the kind of people you think they are?"

"They don't deserve you helping them like that."

Did he have any idea how his words sounded? How selfish and judgmental and even cruel? It was hard to remember this man was her father. There seemed so little love left in him for anyone, much less her.

"That's just it, Dad. They do. And I'm going to help them. In fact, I'm thinking about staying on at Camp True North Springs. Permanently. So if you can't come to grips with that, I'm sorry. I'm sorry for a lot of things. But I'm not going to be one bit sorry if I come up as a match for Matteo or anyone." A wave of sadness overtook her as she walked out of her father's office. It felt as if she was walking out of his life, walking out of her own family.

"Bridget, do not do this!" her father commanded.

She tried to think of how to answer him, but just walked out of the office building in silence instead.

She held the tears at bay until she made it onto the highway down toward Phoenix, then had to pull over and sob. When no more tears would fall, the steady core of sure resolve was left in its wake.

Bridget had come home to North Springs to figure out who she was. What she looked like as her own woman, on her own path. When she dried her eyes and looked in the car's rearview mirror, she liked what she saw. She felt God's steady hand on her back, sending her forward despite the pain and all that was left behind.

"I'm sorry, Dad," she whispered to the glimpse of North Springs in her rearview mirror. "But I'm not sorry at all." She shifted her gaze to her own reflection. "Let's go save a life." If there was any way she could take the test and register before the sun went down today, she'd do it.

After all, saving lives was what nurses were supposed to do. Especially this nurse.

Carson was dropping off some supply orders with Dana when the gate buzzer let out a long, insistent shrill. Before Dana could even rise from her desk, the buzzer hummed again.

"Expecting someone impatient?" he asked

as he looked out the window. A sleek white car sat just outside the gate.

"Nobody." Dana pressed the intercom speaker button. "May I help you?"

"Let me in," the voice on the other end demanded.

"That's not how we do things here. Who am I speaking to?"

"You're speaking to Arthur Nicholson. Let me in. Now."

Dana and Carson exchanged looks. No one expected Arthur Nicholson to ever set foot on camp property as a guest. His current tone spoke more of an invasion. Dana muted the speaker. "Got any idea?"

"Bridget was going to try to talk to him again this afternoon before she headed down into Phoenix." Carson shrugged as a chill of worry rose in his chest. "That doesn't explain why he's here."

Dana pushed the button again. "Bridget isn't here right now, Arthur."

Arthur Nicholson's impatient growl came through loud and clear. "I know that. Open the gate."

Carson returned the puzzled look Dana gave him. "So why is he here?"

"I guess there's only one way to find out."

Dana pressed the button that opened the fence gate. "Come on up to the big house, Arthur."

"I know where to go." Carson watched the car gun through the opening the minute the gate was wide enough. Dust kicked up behind the sedan as it barreled up the drive to pull in front of the house.

Carson tried to muster some shred of hospitality for the hostile man, and mostly failed. No conversation with Arthur Nicholson was ever pleasant, and he sure wasn't here to lend support to the camp. Bridget's father got out of the car like a man on a war path. "I guess we should be thankful most everyone is out at the nature center today?" he offered with an optimism he didn't feel.

"Maybe." Dana pulled herself up to her considerable height and headed for the door. Carson was right behind her. Even though Dana had been a tough city detective in her past, no way was he going to leave her alone with a brute like Nicholson.

She pushed open the door with an admirably gracious smile. "Hello, Arthur. I'm surprised to see you here."

"Let's dispense with the niceties. I want to see Martina Garza."

That was the last thing Carson expected to

hear. Dana, too, from the looks of it. "Martina's had a rough day. She and Matteo are just back from the hospital, and they're resting in their room. Now's not a good time."

The information did nothing to stem Arthur's dark look. "Go tell her I'm here."

Dana stood firm. "I'll do no such thing."

Carson walked up to stand next to Dana, coming just short of putting himself between her and Arthur. "Our guests have a right to their privacy."

"I'll tell her you came by," Dana said with an impressive calm considering the fury radiating off Nicholson. It wasn't hard to see her law enforcement skills come quickly to the surface. "But I'd prefer to know why."

"That's none of your business," Arthur shot back with the trademark air of condescension that had always gotten under Carson's skin.

"I disagree." Carson put every ounce of defiant "don't test me" vibes into his tone.

Arthur dismissed the two of them as if they were a pebble on the sidewalk and started walking toward the converted barns that served as the guest quarters.

Carson dashed ahead of Arthur and put himself directly in the man's path. He thrust his hand toward Nicholson's chest. "The lady asked you a question. And she asked you to come back later." All of his infuriating history with Bridget's father burned in his chest. No matter who he thought he was, or what power he thought he held, the man was not going to get his way here. Not if Carson had any say in it.

"You," Arthur said as if the word left a sour taste in his mouth. The tone said a hundred things at once, none of them good.

"I'm asking you to leave," Dana said in a voice that clearly meant business. "And I *will* call the police if you don't."

Arthur gave her a brief look, then turned toward the buildings and bellowed, "Martina Garza!"

Carson had reached his limit. He wheeled around in front of Arthur and gave him a shove back toward his car.

"Carson!" Dana yelled.

His blood was pounding in his ears and every inch of his arms was ready to take a swing, but Carson fisted his hands and stood right in front of Arthur, growling.

The man's eyes narrowed, and Dana's posture stiffened as Carson heard the guest quarters' door open behind him. Arthur had no right to disturb Martina after the day she'd had. She'd come home exhausted and disheartened. From the looks of things, Matteo's cancer was showing signs of recurrence. They weren't sure yet—there was still a chance—but it wasn't looking good. The last thing she needed right now was whatever reason had made Arthur Nicholson come after her.

Arthur started toward Martina, and Carson's instant response was to grab Nicholson's arm and hold him back. The two scuffled for a minute until Martina surprised everyone by waving Carson off.

No one knew quite what to do as Arthur and Martina stared at each other for a minute. They had to have known each other—Martina and Bridget and Carson had all gone to school around the same years and North Springs wasn't that large a town.

The surprised stillness didn't last long. Arthur jabbed a finger at Martina and growled, "Don't pull my daughter into your problems. How dare you bully her into this wild-goose chase of yours."

"Nobody bullied Bridget into anything," Carson cut in. He knew he wasn't helping, but the way Arthur saw Bridget as being pushed around by people made his blood boil. "Bridget took up the bone marrow drive on her own."

"You stay out of this," Arthur warned, then leveled an even darker glare at Martina. "And you," he said to her, "you put Bridget up to this. People like you are always looking to have someone else bail you out of your problems."

Dana pulled out her cell phone. "That's enough, Arthur."

He ignored her. "Don't think I don't know why you're here," Arthur went on. "What you're trying to do. What you're all trying to do. Well, it won't work. It never has. You're not wanted here. Go home, Martina. You won't get what you want here."

Martina stalked up to Arthur with a ferocity Carson had never seen from the young mother. "Do you know what I want? I want you to admit who you are. Admit what you've denied for years. To me, to my family. Admit it!"

"I will not. Ever."

Suddenly, details were slamming into place, crashing through Carson's mind with a force ten times stronger than the blow of the beam last week. He and Dana exchanged cautious, stunned looks as Arthur and Martina stood squared off at each other with hate in their eyes.

"Admit it!" she shouted. "Admit that you're my father. Admit it!"

Chapter Thirteen

Carson left the mounting drama to Dana and was behind the wheel before the shouting even stopped. He had to find Bridget. If she didn't know the truth, she needed to. Now. And while some might argue this was a matter between Bridget and her father, there was no way he was going to leave that up to a man like Arthur Nicholson. He cared for Bridget too much to do that.

Carson shouted, "Dial Bridget Nicholson!" into his phone as he gunned his pickup truck down the driveway. He half expected Arthur to be coming after him, but in his rearview mirror he could still see Martina, Arthur and Dana arguing.

He banged his hand on the steering wheel when his call to Bridget went to voice mail. He tried to be thankful she was smart enough not to pick up the phone while driving. "Bridget, you need to call me right away. I'm heading toward you, but I'm not quite sure where. Just call me the minute you get this, okay?" After a moment he added, "If your dad calls you, don't take the call until I get there. I'll explain when I see you."

She was on her way to meet with the donor registry people, but Phoenix was a big town. Urgency tangled his thoughts, and he couldn't even remember the name of the organization, although he was sure she'd told him. If God was kind, she wasn't all the way there yet and he could catch her. *Let me get to her before Arthur does.* Then, recognizing the arrogance of that, he pushed out a breath and added, *Or whatever You think is best. You saw this coming. You're still in control, even if I barely am.*

Carson drove into North Springs, circling the square in the hopes she hadn't gone down to Phoenix yet. Her car wasn't there. He checked in the driveway of her parents' house up on the hill, half considering finding Bridget's mother, but that wasn't any better an idea based on Bridget's last conversation with the woman. He'd drive all the way to Phoenix if he had to. He'd be there for her no matter what it took.

Pulling over to the side of the road, he texted her.

Call me as soon as you can. I'm on my way to you. Just tell me where.

He started heading toward the highway that went down to Phoenix, praying he was headed toward Bridget while he waited for her to respond.

She didn't. He could only assume she was still driving. *Come on, Lord*, he prayed. *Keep her safe but get me to her. Before he does.*

His heart leaped when the phone signaled an incoming call, but sank to see it was Dana, not Bridget.

"Are you headed where I think you're headed?" she asked.

"I gotta get to her before he does. If he hasn't already."

"He denied everything," Dana explained. "It got pretty heated. I'm glad no one else was here to see this. I'm glad Matteo didn't see it."

"Is Arthur still there?" Carson asked.

"No, he stormed out of here. He may be after

you, if he thinks you're headed to Bridget. Where are you?"

"I'm on my way to Phoenix. I've got to catch her. I've left a voice mail and a text, but she won't see it if she's driving. I'll have to catch up to where she's headed. What's the name of the place?"

"Give me a minute." Carson heard papers shuffling. "LifeGift. I'll text you the address. I'll get in touch with Mason and let him know what's going on. And say a boatload of prayers."

"I'll need 'em." He clicked off the call, feeling frantic to do something and helpless to know if he was doing the right thing. After all, what he was about to do constituted family meddling of the first order—something he'd accused Arthur of doing for years. Still, something deep and solid in his chest told him he was in Bridget's life for just this moment. When things unraveled on the huge scale they were about to, he was meant to be there for her. He'd take on the burden of telling her what it seemed neither Martina nor Arthur had the courage say.

Martina. Bridget was becoming so fond of her. And now everything the woman said and did had a deeper agenda. How could Bridget help but feel used if all this was true? Even if it wasn't? Carson's desire to protect Bridget surged up with greater force.

He had just plugged the address texted from Dana into his navigation system when his phone signaled a call from Bridget.

"Carson? What's going on?"

Relief filled his chest. "Where are you?"

"I'm at a gas station in Arcosanti. On my way to LifeGift, like I told you. There are two missed calls from my dad and one from my mom on my phone. What's going on?"

She was fifteen minutes away. "Stay where you are. I'm coming to you. And don't answer those calls from your parents." Carson knew, somehow, that Martina's claims could very well be true and that, based on what he knew of Arthur and Teresa Nicholson, they'd go to any lengths to discredit them.

"I don't understand what's going on."

"I'll be there in fifteen minutes. Give me a chance to explain. After that you can do whatever you decide, but I want you to hear this from me." Realizing that came dangerously close to a demand, he added, "Please? Trust me?" He knew she wanted an explanation now, but this was absolutely not the kind of thing to be done over the phone.

"I'll be late for my meeting with LifeGift," she replied. "Is this about that?"

Arthur's opposition to the project suddenly made a world of sense. "Sort of, but believe me, it's that important. Please, Bridget. Wait for me. Please." Carson closed his eyes and pleaded with God to grant him Bridget's trust.

"All right. I'll call LifeGift and wait for you. But, Carson, you're scaring me."

He started the truck and reminded himself getting pulled over for speeding would only make things worse. "Don't be scared. I'll be there. Twenty minutes tops. Hang on, I'm coming."

Bridget stared at her phone after the call disconnected, running her finger down the logs of miltiple calls from her father, one from her mother, and the most recent from Carson. What was going on? What would make Carson plead for her not to listen to whatever her father had to say? Carson must know something she didn't—or had just learned something he hadn't known when she'd left him at camp this morning. None of it made sense, but then again, so much of her life seemed to be shifting in directions she hadn't anticipated. Her finger lingered over the voicemail message from Dad. It was short—not even a minute. Wouldn't it be better to know what she was dealing with? Whatever Carson was barreling down the highway to tell her? And if it was something big—which it certainly had to be, given Carson's tone—wasn't it better to hear it from Dad no matter how harshly he might put it?

Carson had to have a good reason for his request. Keep yourself occupied until he gets here. Bridget pulled her car away from the gas pumps to under the shade of a trio of trees. This far down into the valley, the lush green of North Springs was already transforming into Phoenix's rocky, cactus-strewn landscape. Moving the car took all of one minute.

She called LifeGift, grateful they could easily see her an hour later than planned. That only took two minutes.

It took two more minutes to buy an iced tea from the gas station. All the while her cell phone silently called to her, the single minute of her father's message beckoning. How much harm can one minute do?

When fifteen minutes had gone by and Carson still hadn't appeared, Bridget's willpower was all used up. She stared at the phone, knowing she could no longer resist pressing the icon to play the message. *Be beside me, Lord. Whatever's about to happen, help me trust You already know it.*

She got into the car, locked the doors for no good reason and pressed the play message icon on the screen.

"I'm telling you not to go down there, Bridget," came her father's voice in fierce tones. "Stop listening to these people. It's all lies. You're being used, and you're too naïve to see it." He still wouldn't believe she had her own wisdom to see the world differently than he did. "Carson, Mason Avery, Martina," he went on, "they're all lying to you. Turn around and come home right this instant. Let me set you straight before they fill your head with lies. You owe me that."

Bridget sat there for a moment, trying to take in what she'd just heard. She bristled at the domineering way Dad spoke to her. He volleyed orders as if scolding a child. Even his "Let me set you straight" wasn't a request—it was a demand. And wasn't it telling that he ordered her to come home while Carson was moving heaven and earth to come *to her*? There was the difference between the two men right there. She couldn't deny Carson was growing in ways that seemed to draw her to him. She was coming to see that what she'd thought of as his ongoing lack of direction was actually a compelling groundedness. A sense of his place in the world. A sense she very much felt lacking in herself.

While Dad, on the other hand, only seemed interested in pulling her back to something she no longer was. Her father insisted on shoving her toward his idea of her path in life, with no interest in letting her find it for herself.

And lies? What lies? What was there to lie about in Camp True North Springs or the bone marrow donor drive? There were unknowns, differences of opinion, but no one had given her any reason to think they were lying to her. No one was using her. She was serving, being *of use*, but that was a world of difference from *being used*.

She was so lost in her thought that the sudden tap on her window made her jump. There was Carson, both hands on the glass of her car door window. The mix of sadness, fear and worry in his expression sent a chill skittering up her spine despite the day's heat.

In the instant Bridget opened the door and got out, Carson wrapped his arms around her. "I'm so glad I found you. I'm so glad I could get to you." He put one hand on her cheek in a gesture that definitely crossed the friendship line she'd asked him to respect. Given the grave look in his eyes, she couldn't fault him for that. He cared. He'd never stopped caring.

She followed his gaze down at the phone she still held in her hands. "I've got more missed calls and a voice mail from Dad. And one from Mom."

"Did you listen to it? To him?"

She nodded, still baffled as to what was going on. Especially when Carson looked stricken that she'd played the voicemail despite his plea.

He pulled her to him again, as if trying to shield her from whatever he felt the message held. "I'm sorry. I'm so, so sorry."

Pulling back, she said, "Carson, I still don't get it. Sure, Dad told me not to go to LifeGift, to come home right this instant, and he told me everyone is lying to me. About what? What is going on? What did you think he said?"

Carson took her hand and led her the shady portion of the little cement wall going along the side of the gas station parking lot. He looked so troubled as he motioned for them to sit. If Dad hadn't been so insistent about lies, Bridget would have thought someone had died.

Carson's desperately serious expression sent a band of fear tightening around her lungs.

He spoke slowly, choosing his words carefully. "I don't think Martina may have been entirely truthful about why she's here."

"She's here because her husband was killed, and Matteo is sick. She's here to try to heal, like all of them."

Carson kept his hand around hers. "Whose idea was the bone marrow donor drive?"

She stared at him. "What's that got to do with any of this?"

"Just think back if you can. Was it her idea or yours? It's important."

Bridget's phone rang, and the screen flashed a notification that the call was from Dad. "I'm not going to answer that," she assured him. "Not until you tell me what's going on."

"The drive…" he persisted.

She shrugged. "I don't know, really. We were talking about Matteo's future, about how his remission could go well, or not. She mentioned them recommending she consider a bone marrow transplant, but that that had risks, too. She told me how sad she was no match had turned up in her family because an immediate family match made things so much easier. I guess it's a long shot just pulling from the general population." Something popped up into her mind. "She said she believed, somehow, that Matteo's match was here."

"And your father was dead set against you hosting the donor drive."

"Well, yes, but he's dead set against anything about Camp True North Springs. We went around about it again just before I came here." She put the phone down. "He had the nerve to forbid me to be the first to sign up to be a donor. As if I was a child and needed his permission. He told me I was too naïve to see the truth in how all of you were lying to me." She felt her jaw tighten at the memory of his patronizing tone. "It was pretty awful."

Carson shifted and took both her hands. "It's about to get worse."

Chapter Fourteen

"Worse? How?" The band of fear around Bridget's chest began to tighten. Dad couldn't shut down the camp. He had no control over an organization like LifeGift. And he'd failed in his attempt to rally the town against Mason and Dana. How could he have any power to make it worse? The grip Carson kept on her hands raised her pulse.

"Your dad came up to camp just now."

"But why? He knew I wasn't there. He knew I was headed here."

"He wasn't there to see you. He demanded to see Martina. And he wasn't nice about it."

Bridget could only imagine. Dad had never set foot on Camp True North Springs' property—even to visit her—so he had to be pretty steamed to drive up the mountain. But… "Martina?"

"Oh, he gave Dana a piece of his mind, too. But she wasn't backing down. She told him to leave, said he couldn't see Martina and even threatened to call the police if he didn't leave."

Dana's law enforcement background gave her an iron will. She wouldn't hesitate to wield it, even on Dad. "Did she get him to leave?"

"I think maybe she would have succeeded if Martina hadn't come out of her guest room. They got into it. Fast."

Bridget pulled one hand from Carson's grip to wipe her forehead—or contain her tangled thoughts, she wasn't sure which. "About what? Me?"

"Well, it started out that way. He accused Martina of pulling you into her problems, of using you, all the stuff he's been spouting all along."

Carson was holding something back, reaching for a way to tell her something. Whatever it was, it loomed big and dark. Bridget stood up off the small stone wall and turned to face him. "Carson, just tell me. What happened?"

He took a deep breath. "Martina demanded that your dad admit that he's her father."

She couldn't have heard him right. "What?"

"According to Martina, your dad is her dad. You're related."

It was an ordinary gas station, a patch of pavement and some buildings along the highway leading into Phoenix, but at that moment Bridget felt as if it was the edge of the world. "Martina? Dad is Martina's father? My dad?" It couldn't be. It made no sense at all. It had to be a lie…didn't it?

Carson pulled her back down, and she hit the wall with enough force that she realized she must have been swaying under the weight of her shock. "It's wild, I know," he said softly. "And no one really knows if it's true, but it does explain a few things."

"Why she's back here." Bridget practically choked on the words. Martina could actually be using her as a way to find a match. But that couldn't be. Dad couldn't be right. She wasn't that naïve. She was a good person trying to help a mother and son who'd endured a pair of terrible tragedies.

"Could be. And why your dad was so insistent you not get involved with her."

The facts swarmed around her. "Her match. Well, Matteo's match. If we're related—Dad and me—we could be matches. She said she felt sure Matteo's match was here. That's because *we are* here. If Martina is my half sister, then Matteo is my half nephew."

"All of which might be proved by the match process. They must have kept the secret for decades—if either or both of you matched, the truth might come out."

Dad? Martina's father? Dad with Martina's mother? Dad unfaithful to Mom with a baby—her—at home? The impossibility of it all crashed against her, a flash flood of doubt and denial.

And betrayal. Carson was right—it explained a lot. Dad's rejection of Camp True North Springs was bad enough, but his singular, almost irrational condemnation of helping Matteo?

"He won't help?" she spit out. "That's his *grandson* and he won't help?"

Carson looked lost for words. What words could possibly contain the enormity of what had just unfolded?

"I was ready to help even before I knew I might be one of the only people who could, and he won't? Just to keep a secret?" Betrayal—and something dangerously close to repulsion—came at her in uncontrollable waves.

"Bridget," Carson said with a calmer tone than she wanted him to show, "we don't actually know it's true."

"It is." Some hard, dark and now burning

place deep inside her knew. "I felt drawn to him. I mean, Martina and I weren't that close in school. Dad actually told me not to be friends with her, now that I think about it. But every time I looked at Matteo, I felt…something." Tears of hurt or pain or just plain confusion stung her eyes. "I thought the connection was just my need to help, to make a difference for someone after feeling so—" she scrambled to describe the drifting feeling overtaking her right now "—insufficient on the *Brilliance* or in Anders's family's eyes. But it wasn't just that."

Carson reached up and wiped away the tears she hadn't even realized had begun to fall. "I don't know what to say."

"There isn't anything to say. Martina lied to me about why she's here. Why she planted the idea of my being here. Dad's been lying to me my whole life. And Mom—she has to know. She wouldn't have called me if she didn't know, right? Unless Dad's been lying to her all this time, too." A desperate sob clawed its way out of her. "Everyone's lied to me."

Carson grabbed her shoulders. "Not everyone."

Bridget knew she should receive that for the truth it was. She should respect it, recognize the integrity of the man who just sped down the highway to catch her and be the one to wound her with this shattering truth. Only it was beyond her at the moment. She didn't know what to think or feel or what to do next. It felt as if everything solid had slid out from underneath her.

The great Arthur Nicholson, exposed. All of his harsh, judgmental nature felt doubly sharp and cruel given what she now knew. All his talk about how people's choices make their circumstances—it rang hollow and hypocritical. And yet some fragile and irrational little-girl part of her cried, *He's right. You've been used. Lied to. And you were too naïve to see it.*

She wrapped her hands around her waist because it felt as if she were about to fall to pieces. As if she would literally come undone and spill out like broken glass, useless and scattered.

"Hey. Come back to me. Talk to me, Bridget." Carson's voice sounded far away. "I'm here for you and I'm not going anywhere."

She couldn't find words. She simply fell into his arms, unable to hold herself upright in the landslide overtaking her life.

He held her for a long time.

Carson expected Bridget to dissolve into

sobs, but she never did. He could feel the pain of betrayal rippling through her, but she never came totally undone. Still, she must feel as if her life had been upended. He thought of a dozen things to say, but simply held her and said prayers over the wild turn her life had just taken. He said prayers of thanksgiving, too, that he'd been able to be here for her, to shield her from whatever defensive barbs her father might choose to throw at her right now. It hurt to be the one to tell her what he knew, but he would throw himself on that sword a hundred times for Bridget.

I'd always thought the reason I was at camp was for the families, or myself. But it was for her, to be here for her right now.

"What now?" he asked when she finally pulled away and straightened up.

Bridget looked around the drab little parking lot and gave a weak laugh. "Well, I can't stay here."

"No."

"I need to talk to Martina. And Dad. And Mom." After a moment, she added, "And probably God. Him first, I suppose."

"You know Dana would tell you none of this is a surprise to Him." Carson shrugged. "You gotta admit, the timing is too epic to think any of this was random." He dared to slide his hand into hers, grateful when she tightened her grip. The urge to protect her welled inside him, but from what? And how? There were so many layers to this situation, it was hard to know where to start.

Bridget raised her eyes to his. "You came and told me." She seemed to recognize the effort and commitment behind his race down the mountain. "Thank you for that."

"I knew it would hurt. I wanted to be here for you." *Because I care so much about you*, his heart proclaimed even as he stifled the words. Somehow he'd known, even from that first day when she'd drawn that big, fat, platonic line between them, that if they ever did cross the line, she would need to do it first. But he'd wait. He'd wait for however long it took.

She looked up at the sky. "What *is* the next right thing? There's a million things I could do about all this, but what's the next right thing?" Carson wasn't sure if she was asking God, the clouds, him or just the world in general.

He pulled in a deep breath. "What feels like the next right thing?"

"Not going back up the mountain to yell at Dad," she said. "Although it's tempting." Arthur always seemed to have a hold over her, a control Carson had never found to be about love or protection. He couldn't bring himself to be sad that this seemed to have snapped that unhealthy bond. The world was about to watch Bridget Nicholson step into her own, and he could only be thankful for that despite all the current pain.

"You two are going to have to have this out, I agree. But maybe not today."

"And I need to talk to Martina. I don't think she's lying, Carson. Dad wouldn't be so frightened of her if she was." She shifted on the cement wall to face him, and he could see the gears spinning in her head. "Think about it. The odds against me matching Matteo are unbelievably high. Even among siblings, it's only one in four. And still he thinks a match might let the secret out. Secrets only have that kind of power if they're true."

"And now it's out anyway, whether the donor drive goes through or not. Kind of the way it is with secrets, isn't it? They find a way to the surface no matter how deep you bury them."

"But what about Matteo? He's a pawn in this as much as I am. All these lies shouldn't get the chance to hurt him. Life's hurt him enough already."

He'd never admired Bridget more. The people who were supposed to love her and call her friend had done awful things, and she was thinking about the welfare of the little boy at the center of it all.

Bridget straightened. "Nothing's changed for him. He's still got leukemia. But a bone marrow donor might still be his best shot." She looked at her watch. "I can still make that appointment at LifeGift."

"Are you sure?"

"No. But at the moment, it's what feels like the next right thing. I'm going down to Phoenix. I'm keeping that appointment and taking that test."

"No, you're not," he replied.

Her eyes flashed. "What do you mean by that?"

"*We're* going down to Phoenix so you can keep that appointment and take that test. I'm going with you." When she looked at him in surprise, he added, "I'm halfway down the mountain now anyway, I might as well go the whole way down with you."

He watched her consider fighting him on this and gave her his best "I mean it" glare. He did mean it. He meant a whole lot more than just driving her down into the valley and the city, whether she knew it or not.

After a long moment, she said, "Thanks."

"You shouldn't have to do this alone. Any of this."

"Okay."

Carson stood up. "Grab your stuff and get in the truck. I'll go arrange to leave your car here for a few hours while we get down and back. You can call Dana and fill her in while I drive."

She nodded, a grateful look filling her features. He started walking toward the gas station office then turned around. "But only if you're sure. You don't have to do any of this. Not today, maybe not even for a while. Nobody would fault you if you took some time to make sense of all of this."

She shook her head. "This feels like the next right thing. Maybe it's the thing that will help me make sense of all this. After all," she added, her voice cracking a bit, "he's my nephew. Well, half nephew, anyway."

As he walked into the little station building, Carson could barely believe the smile that crept onto his lips. Matteo would never be a half nephew to Bridget. That woman had never done anything halfway in her life.

Chapter Fifteen

Fiona Stewart wore a long braid of silver-gray hair and had bright eyes that defied her advanced years. "I'm happy you want to host a donor drive to help this boy. We need all the donors we can get. But I want to make sure you understand—it is a long shot that anyone in North Springs will be the match Matteo needs."

Maybe not as much as you'd think, Bridget thought. *Certainly not as much as when I left the camp this morning.* Had it been mere hours since her world had turned upside down? Life floated in a surreal bubble that would surely pop—more like explode—the minute she went back up into North Springs.

Fiona slid a form across the table. "I know you're here to help Matteo. But to be clear, you're signing up for the public registry. That means we will call you if you match a total stranger anywhere. North Springs or North Dakota."

Bridget pulled the form to her and picked up the pen. "I understand."

"You can save a life, but it may not be Matteo's."

Bridget signed the form. "Who'd say no to that?"

Fiona gave a sad smile. "You'd be surprised. Everyone wants to be a hero for someone they know. Not so much for a total stranger you may never meet."

"You got another one of those forms?" Carson asked. Bridget felt her eyebrows raise. She hadn't expected this.

Carson cocked his head to one side as if it were no big deal. "Like the woman said, who'd say no to saving a life?"

It was a huge deal. After her father's blatant rejection, Carson's participation felt enormous. A foothold against the day's onslaught of disappointment and betrayal.

Fiona produced a second set of forms. "The world needs more people like you. There's so much more we could be doing with a larger pool of donors. I know the odds seem astronomical to help Matteo, but the odds of helping the thousands of people who need this get better with each new person signing up."

"If we could get every one of the camp families and people in North Springs…" Bridget began, feeling a welcome sense of equilibrium after having been thrown so far off balance.

"*When* we get every one of the camp families and most of the people in North Springs," Carson amended.

His choice of the word "most" seemed aimed at her father. Bridget still couldn't process all she'd learned. Not only did her father have a big secret, but he was also willing to keep it hidden at the expense of Matteo's life. To risk that on the long-shot possibility of him matching Matteo? Or her? Fear really did make people behave in awful ways.

As it stood, Bridget didn't know whether to hope she could be a match, or pray she wasn't. *I can only ask You to provide the match that's needed, Lord. I'm going to have to leave the who up to You.*

The procedure was surprisingly simple: a cheek swab put into a vial and shipped off to a testing lab. The rest of the visit was spent ironing out the details of hosting the donor drive in North Springs.

"We can even come up to the camp and register your families there," Fiona said, "if it's too much trouble for them to make the trip down into North Springs."

"No," Bridget replied, "I'd really like everyone to do it together. I'd like people to see each other helping." *I'd like Dad to see all these people who have lost so much generously offer what he's refusing to give.*

She wasn't proud of her current dark feelings toward her Dad. She couldn't say if this wall of betrayal and disappointment destroyed their relationship forever. Bridget felt lost, caught between facts and feelings whirring around her too fast to make any sense.

Once they stepped outside the LifeGift offices, Bridget was almost surprised to see that the world kept on going, as though everything was fine and her life hadn't been flipped upside down.

"That's two." Carson gave a tentative smile and held up a pair of fingers. "Who knows how many more donors you'll have signed up before all this is over?"

"I don't think this is going to be over anytime soon," she said, staring up at the mountainside in the direction of North Springs. She was going to have to go back up there and face this sooner or later. She didn't feel strong enough at the moment, but lingering down here in the valley felt hot and useless.

Carson gave her elbow a tender touch. "How are you?"

"Confused. Hurt. Wondering what else I don't know. What else isn't true?" She hated how she questioned everything now.

"Do you still think this was the next right thing?"

"Yeah." The certainty in her voice startled Bridget slightly. "This was a good thing before, and it's still a good thing. It's just complicated by a lot of other things for me now."

"You just made a difference, you know. Maybe for Matteo, maybe for someone else. You can be proud of that, no matter how we ended up here." Carson led her toward the truck. "It's up to you when we go back. We don't have to until you're ready. And you can decide if we go to the camp or to town."

Bridget welcomed the compassion in his eyes. "You mean do I confront Martina or my dad first. I don't know which hurts more. My dad's been lying to me my whole life, but Martina used me."

Carson stopped. "You don't actually know that yet."

Bridget shot him a look. "Martina has no reason to lie about this. She put the idea of coming here in my head. She slipped in the idea of the bone marrow donation. She planted all those seeds while keeping it from me that we were half sisters. I'm hurt, and I don't know what I'm going to do about that yet, but I don't doubt that it's true."

It came to her, at that moment, as she talked through the facts with him. "I start with Dad. Give him a chance to own up to this. I'm not sure I can go any further if he won't."

Carson suggested, pointing toward a small café just down the block from where they were standing, "How about we start with food? Have you eaten since breakfast?"

"Just that bottle of iced tea at the gas station."

He started walking. "This is too big a crisis to deal with on an empty stomach. Let's get something to eat. It'll give you a chance to think through what comes after that." Carson nodded toward the mountain. "That mess will all still be waiting when we get there."

"'Mess' is the right word," she agreed. "I suppose I should eat."

"A good sandwich doesn't solve the world's problems, but it sure helps."

Bridget wasn't sure how he could make a joke on a day like this, but the sorry attempt at humor soothed her somehow. His steady presence made the day feel less enormous, less off balance. Life wouldn't right itself anytime soon, but maybe she wouldn't have to solve it all alone. Then again, could it be solved? The secret that had been revealed today couldn't be put back, ever.

"Thank you for making sure I didn't face this alone. You're a good friend."

"That's me, a good friend." The flash of disappointment in his eyes told her he wasn't entirely in favor of the classification.

Despite her growing feelings, Bridget couldn't add a relationship with Carson back into the mix. She was in no shape to make any wise emotional choices right now, grasping at the support he offered whether it was wise or not. "I'm grateful—this can't have been easy." She knew she wasn't giving him what he wanted.

"You mean a lot to me, B. I hope you know that. And you're going to get through this, however it turns out. You know what they say up there, 'You've got what it takes to get through this.'"

It was something the staff said to camp families all the time, according to Mason. "Tell them we believe they have what they need to keep healing."

Carson was telling her the same thing. The hard part was going to be believing it.

The ride back to Bridget's car was too quiet. Carson had so many things he wanted to say and a pile of actions he wanted to take. Still, he knew it was wrong to get out in front of this before Bridget. If he swooped down and gave in to his urge to play protector here, he'd be no better than what Arthur had done in convincing Bridget to break it off with him. His head knew that, but his heart and his gut were beyond sore at the idea of someone like Arthur looking down on him, finding him lacking in the moral and social standing to make a life with Bridget. Knowing what he knew now, Carson didn't think Arthur held the right to look down on him or anyone.

As Carson pulled next to Bridget's waiting car at the little gas station, he dared a question. *The* question, actually.

"What are you going to do now?" She'd gone back and forth on her next action all through their meal. He sensed she'd come to a decision on the drive, and he wanted to know what it was. He wanted to know how he could help. Even if this situation didn't propel their relationship into something more—and there was no guarantee that it would—Carson would be the friend to help her through this.

"I've changed my mind, and I'm going to see Martina. I want to hear what she has to say before I talk to my father." The decisiveness in her voice sounded much more like Bridget than the wounded indecision she'd been groping her way through since they'd last sat in this parking lot. "I'm angry that she kept this from me. It feels like a lie. But it feels like more truth than what I'll get from Dad—if that makes any sense."

He nodded, fighting the urge to pull her close the way he had earlier. "It makes a whole lot of sense to me." He dared to add, "I'll be happy to come with you when you do, if you want. You shouldn't have to do it alone."

He knew her answer just by the way she gathered up her things. "No, I do. You've been wonderful today, really, and I really do appreciate everything. This next part just has to be on me."

He couldn't stop himself. "Are you sure? I mean she knows I know. I was there when she confronted your dad." He had no reason to be hurt over the fact that she wasn't letting him into this hugely crucial moment in her life. He'd already been deeply involved—he'd been the one to tell her. He didn't want her to take the next steps without him. *You have to let her do it how she needs to,* he commanded himself.

He said it over and over as he watched Bridget get in her car and drive up the mountain to face her challenges. *Let her do it how she needs to.* He continued to think it as he waited ten minutes after she'd gone, just to make sure he didn't do anything foolish like follow right behind her.

He said it all the way back to North Springs and onto the street where Arthur Nicholson lived, and while he stared at the house on the hill. He stood on the sidewalk and told himself not to go bang on the door and do something he'd surely regret.

It was almost working. Carson had his hand on the truck door handle ready to get back inside…until Arthur pulled open the front door and gave him a look so black it burned from clear across the street.

They stared at each other for an angry moment. Carson told himself there was nothing to be gained in getting into this with Arthur. It didn't help.

"You told her what that woman accused me of." Arthur ground the words out as he came down off the porch.

That's right, Carson said silently to himself. *Come down off your high perch on the hill and own up to it in front of me.* "I did." He hoped Arthur heard the complete lack of apology in his tone.

Arthur walked toward him. "You had no right."

Carson held his ground. "Maybe that's how you see it."

"You had no business repeating that lie to Bridget, to put her through that. It was for me to set her straight before Martina filled her head with that nonsense."

Bridget was right about one thing: Arthur was more than ready to decide for her what was right rather than let her decide for herself. Bridget was so capable, had so much more grace to give the world than Arthur ever gave her credit for. How could a father, even in the name of protection, so underestimate his daughter?

Carson decided to cut straight to the point. "Is it a lie? What Martina said?"

"Of course, it's a lie!" Arthur shot back.

"Because it explains a lot if it's true. How

much you fight the camp. Why you forbade her to sign up to donate bone marrow. Which she's already done, by the way. So whatever you were hoping to keep hidden by that, it isn't happening."

Arthur's eyes narrowed to angry slits. "And I expect you egged her on. You probably drove her down there yourself. You were always first in line to get her to defy me. You were never any good for her. You're still no good for her. Really, what have you changed about yourself? I heard Gordon Jacobs offered you an apprenticeship and you turned him down. That's all you want to be? A maintenance man? Do you think I want my daughter with a *janitor*?"

His words cut loose the last of Carson's control. "Cut me down all you want, Arthur, but it won't change what's happening. You're so busy managing Bridget to meet your expectations, you don't even see how you're losing her. You're *losing* her, Arthur, and that has nothing to do with me."

"It has *everything* to do with you," Arthur fired back. "You think you've got her back, and so you're ready to fill her head with lies about us so you can get what you want." One hand jabbed toward the mountain where the camp lay. "I knew this would happen if we let her go up there. I should have stopped her."

"She's a grown woman, Arthur. You don't get to stop her from doing anything. Don't you expect me to sit back and watch you hurt her. *Again.* I won't do it." He took a step closer to Arthur even though he knew it was a bad idea. He was too close to the boiling point to show any restraint. "You can hate me all you want. Cut me down by whatever sorry measurements you use. You can't hurt me because I don't care what you think."

"You don't care what anyone thinks—that's as clear as it's ever been."

Arthur's derision no longer meant anything to him. "I should have stood up to you the first time. And that's on me. But I won't back down now. I *will* protect Bridget. Even from you, if I have to. Only, I don't think I'll have to, because she can take care of herself."

Arthur huffed. "Clearly, she can't, or she wouldn't be up there pretending she hasn't just thrown her future away."

"She has *not* thrown her future away," Carson nearly shouted. "But you'll throw away your future with her if you keep lying and controlling her. Tell her the truth, Arthur. You'll lose her if you don't." He put his hand to his forehead. "Why am I even trying to do this? You've never done anything but look down on me."

Arthur puffed his chest up like an angry bull. "That's because my daughter has always deserved better than the likes of you."

There was no sharper blade for Arthur to thrust into Carson. "You're wrong. I love her. I always have. I probably always will. And if she decides that's not enough, it'll be because *she's* decided it. Not because you decreed it."

"I'll not have you—"

Carson cut him off, ready to say everything that had been building up inside him for years. "If I have to fight you for her, I will. And it'll be a fight because *you* made it one, not because I wanted it. But since demands seem to be all you know, then I will demand this—admit the truth to Bridget. She already knows it, whether you're willing to admit it or not."

"She's been fooled—"

Carson refused to let him get a word in. "You owe her that honesty. She deserves the truth. I don't care how much you think it hurts you. Or your precious upstanding reputation. Because if you ask me, your honesty is about the only thing you can give her to save any kind of relationship with her."

Arthur started in on whatever response he was ready to hurl, but Carson refused to listen as he turned to leave. He ignored the man's angry words at his back and got into the truck.

Only when he was halfway up the mountain did he realize the most dangerous words he'd said aloud to Arthur. *I love her. I always have. I probably always will.*

Followed, like a roll of thunder after a bolt of lightning, by what he had said next. *And if she decides that's not enough...*

Chapter Sixteen

It was dark by the time Carson drove through the camp gates. It felt as if he'd been gone for years instead of hours.

He was glad to see Bridget's car in the parking lot, and thankful to see the circle of camp families gathered around the firepit as if today had been an ordinary day. "Ordinary" was the last word to describe today. As he hauled his weary body—and, truth be told, his weary soul—out of the truck, Carson found he couldn't tell if the words "good" or "bad" could describe today, either.

That was up to Bridget.

The last hours had amplified his feelings for her, pulling all the old longings to the surface in fierce waves. He ached to be near her, knowing what she was going through. Scanning the faces around the circle of firelight, he couldn't see Martina or Matteo. What did that mean? Dana caught his eye, her expression as mixed as his own emotions. She held up a hand to pause whatever Doug Jennings was saying to her and rose to come toward him in the parking lot.

"Whopper of a day," she said with a heavy exhale.

"Where is she?"

Dana glanced back to the house. "In her room. She and Martina were in the conference room for two hours."

"And?"

Dana shrugged. "I don't know. I haven't seen either of them since. I thought maybe they needed space." She offered a small hopeful smile. "But maybe she'd like to see you."

Carson swallowed. "Maybe not."

"What do you mean?"

He rubbed the back of his neck, as if the regret sent an itch up his spine. "I went to see Arthur."

Dana's smile faded quickly. "Oh, no. Carson, you didn't."

"I did. I said everything I've been burning to tell that man for years. Evidently today was the day everything came out into the open." When Dana opened her mouth to tell him what he already knew, he went on, "I know, I know, now I'm just as guilty of sticking my nose in where it doesn't belong as he is. But I just couldn't stand the thought of him controlling what she knows and what she ought to think. I told him if he wanted any hope of saving a relationship with Bridget, he owed her the truth."

"You're not wrong," Dana replied. "But that might not have been the best strategy. Or timing."

"I know."

They both looked toward the house. "You'd better go talk to her," she said quietly.

He knew that. She deserved the truth from him as much as he'd insisted on it from her father. "I said one more thing to Arthur I probably shouldn't have."

Dana's blond eyebrow raised. "Only one?"

The hand strayed to the back of his neck again, the night suddenly stifling. "Well, I said a lot of things I probably shouldn't have. Or maybe things I ought to have said long before this."

"Like?"

Carson looked at Dana. "I told him I had always loved his daughter and still did."

She gave a slow nod as she absorbed that.

"Well, then, you'd *definitely* better go talk to her."

He nodded back, pulled in a deep breath and turned toward the house. "Send up a prayer or two for me?"

The hopeful smile returned and she touched Carson's arm. "Twelve…maybe twenty."

I'll take all I can get, Carson thought as he mounted the stairs of the big house porch. Bridget's room and the infirmary were near the back, and he could see the light spilling out into the hallway.

And he could hear her voice. "Absolutely not! How can you ask me that?" Hurt filled the sharp tone of her words. "How can you expect me to believe anything you say right now, Dad?"

Of course, Arthur would try to talk to Bridget before he did now. He'd take Carson's impulsive confrontation and paint it in the worst possible light—as manipulation rather than care. He'd made a mess of it, all right.

Should he just walk away and try again tomorrow? No, Carson couldn't bear to leave Bridget twisting in the wind of whatever Martina and Arthur had said to her in the last hours. She'd never deserved to be thrust in between their conflict, however eager they seemed to put her there.

He wouldn't stay away tonight, even if things got messy. Well, mess*ier*.

Carson walked into the wedge of light thrown by the open door and waited. The look on Bridget's face the moment she turned and noticed him said everything. Her eyes, so full of wounded tenderness before, blazed hard and cold. "He just walked in." Her words as icy and cold as her eyes.

Bridget didn't look one bit ready to forgive him for going to Arthur instead of letting her go first. *What do you know,* he thought with an absurd clarity at the sharp pang in his chest, *you really can feel your heart break.*

Bridget ended the call without even saying goodbye to her father. She glared at Carson as she tossed the phone onto her bed. "How could you do that?"

Carson swallowed back his answer of "I was trying to protect you." That was too much like something Arthur would say. He stayed silent.

"You're no better than he is."

Nothing she said could have wounded him more.

"You put yourself in the middle of this. You told me before he could. You went to him before I could. Why are the two of you tackling my problems as if I can't handle them on my own? Why is no one here letting me make the choices *I* want about any of this?"

Carson put his hand out. "I shouldn't have gone."

"No, you shouldn't have. I told you I was going to talk to him after I heard what Martina had to say. Not that you listened."

He deserved that. "I thought if I could—"

"You thought you could fix this for me," she cut in. "Face down Dad better than I could, maybe even get back at him for all the ways he hurt you. How much of North Springs heard the two of you hurling insults at each other? Outside in the street, Carson? You had it out with my dad on the sidewalk in front of their house?"

"I was trying to go inside. Actually, I was trying *not* to go inside, to stop myself from going inside, when he came out and…" Carson halted, sure that anything more he said would start to sound like a child whining.

"Did you think I couldn't handle confronting Dad? Do I look that weak to you?"

She was badly hurt, torn open and raw from the pain of the day. He knew that was what drew the accusations she was flinging at him. But she wasn't entirely wrong. He'd convinced himself he'd stepped in out of care—love, actually. But it was also out of fear. Fear that Arthur would somehow succeed in pulling Bridget away. He couldn't bear that. Not again.

There was only one thing to say. "I was wrong."

"Yes, you were." She glared at him. "I don't need Dad's opinion to tell me that." She closed her eyes, and Carson noticed her lashes were wet. Who had made her cry? Arthur? Martina? Both?

"I lost my cool," he went on. "I'm sorry I went to him before you. I told him to tell you the truth, that I was sure he'd lose you if he went on…"

She held up her hand to silence him, eyes still closed. "Stop. Just stop."

Now he was the one in danger of losing her if he went on. He'd meddled, which was the last thing on earth she wanted from him or anyone right now.

"Go away," she said wearily. "I just want everyone to go away."

Carson had no choice but to do just that. He could say a hundred prayers tonight and it wouldn't come close to matching the storm of regret that swirled around him as he walked out into the dark night.

* * *

Bridget knocked softly on Martina's guest room door late into the evening.

"I'm leaving in the morning," Bridget announced when Martina opened the door with a cautious look. "I can't stay here."

Martina looked shocked for a moment then nodded slowly.

"I want you to know," Bridget continued, "that if I'm a match for Matteo—I know it's an incredibly long shot—but if I do match, I'll donate. None of this is his fault."

Tears welled up in Martina's eyes. "*Gracias*. I just…"

She didn't want to draw this out. This was going to hurt and was best done quickly. "You just should have told me the truth in the first place. I'm not my father. I'm not…*our* father." The last two words felt as if they yanked the ground out from underneath her.

"You believe me."

She did. "He insisted that it was all lies, but yes, I believe you." It *was* true. She just *knew* it, even though she couldn't exactly say how. Still, that wasn't what she'd come to say. "You didn't have to trick me into helping you. I would have done it all along."

Martina flinched slightly at the cruel word,

but Bridget felt as if everyone was tricking her, manipulating what she knew and which actions she could take. "LifeGift will know how to find me when the test results come in." What was it Fiona had said? Some people come in wanting to help someone they know, but they lose interest if it's helping a stranger. Even though she knew Matteo and now knew the reason for the inexplicable pull she felt toward the boy, the layers of deceit made him feel like a stranger. That made no sense. Maybe nothing about this would make sense anytime soon. At least not here.

"Where are you going?" Martina asked.

Not home. That's all she really knew right now. She needed to put a lot of distance between herself and any of this. Coming to Camp True North Springs had seemed so perfect mere weeks ago, but now it lacked all the clarity she'd hoped to gain. If anything, her vision was murkier than ever. Nicholsons weren't ever supposed to be quitters, but here she was about to quit her job after quitting her job after quitting her engagement. "I don't know where, just not here."

"Don't leave," Martina pleaded. "I didn't handle this right. I should have been straight with you from the beginning. But that's on me. People think you're great here. Don't make everyone else pay for my mistakes."

Mistakes. Bridget felt like she was drowning in other people's mistakes at the moment. All too afraid of the mistakes she'd make herself given how wounded she felt. Staying here was asking her soul to skip across a minefield—something was bound to be blown to bits.

Martina looked around as if the staff and guests might appear out of the darkness. "Have you told anyone else yet? Dana and Mason? Carson?"

"They're next." She would slip a note under Mason and Dana's door, asking to meet first thing in the morning, planning to be fully packed with her car loaded before breakfast. She'd say a quick goodbye to the families, get into the car before anyone could talk her out of it and then probably cry her way onto the highway in whatever direction seemed best at the time.

Martina sighed. "I wish you wouldn't go."

"We all wish for a lot of things."

Martina reached out a hand. "God go with you, Bridget. I'm sorry. For all of it."

Bridget believed her, but it wasn't enough. Maybe someday, with a bit of time, it would be. Maybe they'd find a way to nurture the tangled family connection they now had. She just couldn't do it now. Not yet. She suspected Martina wanted to hug her, but Bridget only squeezed Martina's hand. It was an insufficient response, but there was no helping it.

After Martina shut the door, Bridget looked up at the sky for a moment, grasping for whatever it was she'd need to go and knock on Carson's door. Courage? Conviction? After making her way over to his quarters located at the end of one of the barns, she pulled in one last deep breath and tapped lightly on his door.

He yanked the door open immediately, looking ragged and worried. He stared at her so directly that she lost the words she'd rehearsed to say.

"Don't. Don't you leave."

How had he known? "I... I can't stay."

"Yes, you can." He grabbed her hand. "It's hard, I know. And messy, and I can't even imagine how much it hurts, but, Bridget, please don't leave. Us. Them. Me."

"I can't stay here. Dad will just keep at it, and how am I supposed to act toward Matteo and Martina, and soon everyone will know..." The reasons to flee rose up like a flash flood around her, too fast and too strong. "I can't."

"Look around you," Carson said, his free hand waving toward the compound around them. "This place is filled with people who know what it's like to feel overwhelmed.

Going someplace else won't help. It'll just be the *Brilliance* all over again."

Bridget flinched at the jab. "That's a lousy thing to say."

"You said it yourself. You told me you went to the *Brilliance* for all the wrong reasons. Seeing the world was just your fancy way of running away from home."

She pulled away from him. "I don't have to stay. It's too hard to stay."

"Sometimes staying is the hardest thing there is." The blue of his eyes turned more ice than sky. "Every square inch of this town hurt when you left me. Every look, every kind comment, every boast about your bright new future scraped me raw. Your dad's smug, victorious looks—when he dared to look at me at all— hurt. But you know what? I slogged through it. I thought if I could heal from it here, with all the reminders of you all over the place, then I'd be okay no matter what. Who was I kidding? I didn't heal at all."

He'd never spoken like this. He'd been careful and kind before, and now he was cracking things wide open. Making her see the pain she'd left him behind to wade through. Funny how wrong she'd been to think he'd had the easier time of it.

Carson hadn't let go of her hand. "And then you came back. You walked through that gate, and everything broke open again. And you asked to be *friends*." The word was edged with pain. "I can't be friends with you, B. I don't have it in me to do anything but love you. Can't you see that?"

She did see that. She'd ignored it from the first day, telling herself it was more important to prove she could be her own person and defy her father's ridiculous prejudices about this place.

She merely nodded a reply, finding any other answer too dangerous for words. She knew he loved her. She just didn't believe love was enough. It hadn't been with Anders, and what her father called love fell far short of what she needed. For all its power, love couldn't be enough to stand against all the things coming at her.

Her silence wounded him, she knew that. "The donor drive is Saturday." He threw up his hands, the angry frustration returning. "Just how are we supposed to do that without you?" She could see it bothered him that he had to resort to something so practical, that his plea alone wasn't enough to keep her there.

"You've already registered. You and Dana and Mason can pull it off."

"Without you?"

She knew he was talking about more than the donor drive. "I've already told Martina that if I'm a match, I'll donate. I don't need to be here to do that."

Carson glared at her. "You can't start this and walk off. And the session's almost over. You can't quit on this. The Bridget I know isn't that kind of person." After a pause, he added, "Don't let your dad turn you into that kind of person." He softened again. "Bridget, don't leave. Just tell me what I have to do to keep you from leaving."

Stop looking at me like that. He was wearing down her resistance. She was so off balance that if she gave in to her growing feelings— even the slightest bit—she'd fall as hard and as fast as the last time. Already, despite her reservations and the hurt, her heart was pulled toward him. It had been for weeks. *I can't risk it. I'm not strong enough.*

"I mean it. I can't stay here." Staying would mean living under the shadow of her father's deception and attempts to control her. She craved distance—and lots of it—until she felt strong enough to stand firm. Leaning on Carson's support would make her weak. She couldn't be weak, not now.

"You can," Carson pressed. "You only think you can't. I see how strong you are now. Let me help you see it for yourself."

No. I can't let you close again. She could sneak off right now. Steal away in the dark before anyone could talk her out of it.

"Look," Carson continued, "just give it twenty-four hours. That's all. Just one day more. It's been too much of a day to think this all the way through now. Just let the sun go down on this one more time, okay? Give yourself and God time to shake things out. And if you can't stay all the way through the drive, through the end of the session, well, that'll be it."

The tender urgency in his tone made her suddenly feel so tired. Exhausted, to be honest. Maybe just a little while longer. "Maybe."

Relief filled Carson's features. "Besides, the flower ceremony is tomorrow. You really need to see that. It's everything amazing about this place all wrapped up into one thing."

"So everybody keeps saying." People spoke of the Camp True North Springs flower ceremony with awe. She'd forgotten how much she'd wanted to see that.

A strong woman could tough it out one more day, right? "Okay."

Chapter Seventeen

Wednesday morning, Mason and Carson stood on the small dock that jutted out a little into the camp pond. They'd been replacing a board to get the structure ready for the event taking place on its banks later that afternoon.

"She hasn't moved since the last time you looked," Mason said, patiently waiting for Carson to turn back from his repeated glances toward the hillside a ways away.

"She went up there after breakfast and hasn't come down."

Mason shoved the board into place and handed Carson the box of nails. "Good place to think."

"Should she be up there all by herself all this time?" Carson shielded his eyes from the blaring sun and tried to get a better glimpse of

Bridget. "Does she have some of those water bottles she's always nagging us to drink? Should I bring her one?"

"What you should do is leave the woman alone to sort through things. This is Bridget you're talking about. She can take care of herself." He took the box of nails back from Carson. "You really are far gone over her, aren't you?"

There seemed little point in denying it. "Yeah."

"Have you told her?"

Carson shook his head. "Worse. I told her father. Right after he called me a janitor. And a slacker for not taking Gordon up on his offer."

Mason raised one eyebrow. "Arthur called you a slacker?"

"Well, he didn't use that word. But the meaning came through loud and clear. So I called Gordon this morning and set up a meeting over coffee to talk things over."

"Don't go doing this just because Arthur cut you down. That's the exact wrong way to go about this." Mason gave him a steady look. "And you're not a janitor. You are a valued member of the camp team. Fine just where you are."

"But I'm not fine. I realized, driving home from that scene with Arthur, that the reason it got under my skin was the grain of truth in it." Carson sat back down on the dock. "When Bridget left, I had to prove her wrong, you know? Somehow, I decided to do that by not making anything of myself. Going out of my way to just wander and barely get by. I think I figured it would let me off the hook."

Mason sat down, as well. "There's no hook. The only measurement worth worrying about is your own. And God's—that matters, too. But I don't believe the Almighty cares about what's on your résumé. I'm all for you improving your skills, but making this about Bridget, or Arthur, would be a mistake." Mason looked toward the big house, a smile filling his features as he caught sight of his wife. "The woman worth having is the one who loves the man, not the title."

"That's just it," Carson replied. "I think maybe I *do* want this. I was just afraid to want it—if that makes any sense. It just stumps me that the three people to help me see it were Gordon, Arthur—" he looked up toward Bridget's silhouette on the hill "—and her." His heart pulled at him just catching sight of her. "I want to be better for her, Mason. For me, too, but to be the person she thought I could be. Maybe she had to go away and come back for me to see it." Carson shook his head. "It's all a mess in my head right now."

"Have you prayed about it? All of it?"

"I was up half the night doing just that. I wish I could say I came away with a boatload of clarity, but all I figured out was to call Gordon and talk to him. And do whatever I can for her."

"Those are pretty good, if you ask me. But maybe you ought to tell Bridget how you feel." Mason picked the hammer back up. "I mean admitting your feelings to Arthur before you told them to her was probably the worst thing you could have done."

Carson blew out a breath and stared up at the sky. "He made me so angry. He was treating her as if she couldn't make her own decisions. I thought if I could just make him see—"

"You thought if you could just protect her from it all," Mason cut in, "which is probably exactly what Arthur was thinking. You know that's how she sees it. Why she's not exactly... grateful you did what you did."

"Not 'exactly grateful'? She's furious."

"She's got a right to be. You messed up."

"Don't I know it."

Mason set a nail and hammered it in. "So maybe the next right thing is to apologize?"

"I did. Over and over." Bridget looked so far away up on that hillside, so ready to slip out of his grasp. "If she leaves... Mason, I'm not sure I can watch her walk away again." Now that Bridget—this new, amazingly strong Bridget—had come back into his life, the fear of losing her gripped him like barbed wire. Made him want to be the kind of man she deserved. And that, he realized, was far more about how he saw himself than how Arthur saw him.

Mason sank the last nail into the board. "So you love her?"

"Yeah, I do. Still. More."

"And you told her that?"

Carson tried to recall if he'd put the overwhelming flood of feelings he'd had when she knocked on his door last night into actual words. "I think I told her she couldn't ask me to be just friends."

"That's not the same thing."

Carson stood up. "I should just go up there right now."

Mason grabbed his ankle. "Hang on. Much as I'm in your corner here, I think maybe you ought to wait a bit. You need to get your own thoughts together as well as give her the space to do the same. Talk to her after the ceremony."

The ceremony wasn't for four more hours. Carson didn't feel like he could hold out that long. "What if she leaves?"

"Then she leaves. You don't get to make that choice for her. Love—real love—isn't control. If you don't know that, you're no better than Arthur."

The power of that truth sunk like a blade into Carson's chest. "I messed this up by trying to fix everything for her, didn't I? Mason, how do I make this better?"

Mason sighed. "You don't. You're going to have to leave this one up to God and Bridget. At least until later."

Carson stared at Bridget still perched on a rock looking out across the valley. It felt like the sorriest of details that she was facing away from him. "How do I wait until later?" He seemed unable to take the pathetic pleading tone out of his voice.

Mason gathered up the tools. "Why don't you go build the garden wall? Put all your strength and worry into that for now. Pray. Ask God to show you when Bridget's ready to talk to you—or, more likely, she'll show you herself. But whatever you do, let it be her call."

Carson never felt less in control in his life. He realized, however, that there was no other way to let this play out than to let it play out. *I'm hanging on by a thread here, Lord. Don't let me fall.*

Sara Lohan grabbed her knee as she lumbered up the small hill on the edge of the property toward where Bridget had been sitting. "Don't ever get old," the woman said with a moan. "It hurts too much."

Bridget found that a poignant remark from a woman who'd known so much emotional pain. "You're far from old, Sara. I hope I have your strength and spunk at your age."

Sara made it to the top of the hill and arched her back. "At my age, everything feels uphill." She gave a soft chuckle. "Even the downhill parts."

The resilient souls Bridget had met here were a constant source of inspiration. Life really did go on after a terrible setback. She just never expected to get such a personal lesson in that truth while she was here.

"I can see this spot from my room." She smirked as she handed Bridget a water bottle. "Here, our camp nurse says to drink these."

"Thanks."

"Want to talk about it?"

The question surprised Bridget. "About

what?" Everyone had been gone on a hike when things had erupted between her father and Martina. Sara couldn't know about what had happened, could she? A chill icier than the water in the bottle trickled down Bridget's spine.

"About whatever's been keeping you up here for hours."

When Bridget pasted an "I'm fine" look on her face, Sara went on to say, "One of the things about having your life come apart at the seams is that you get pretty good at seeing it in other people." She settled down onto the rock next to Bridget's. "The whole 'club nobody wants to join' thing."

There seemed little point in denying it to someone with Sara's perceptive eyes. "I don't want to involve you. You and Daniel are here for your own respite."

"Sometimes talking about it with a total stranger helps more than hashing it out with someone who knows all the history."

"You're not a total stranger." In fact, Sara was one her favorite guests at the camp. The children were adorable and heartwarming, but there was something soft and solid in Sara. A deep and hard-won wisdom.

Sara leaned back as if she had all the time in the world to wait.

Eventually, Bridget drew in a breath. "I learned a big secret this week. One that changes everything."

"I take it, from your expression, that it doesn't change everything in a good way."

Bridget simply shook her head. "Not in a good way" was an understatement.

"We give secrets a lot of power. More than they're meant to have, I think." She glanced at Bridget. "Do you know the way to disarm a secret, how to take its power away?"

"How?"

"You speak it. You drag it out into the open and let the light shrivel it up. Sometimes you have to be careful—people get hurt—but the dark can hurt you just as much. Maybe more."

Sara's words had the ring of truth. "I suppose so."

"Would it help if I told you a secret? One that held me down for a long time?"

Bridget wasn't sure she had earned that kind of trust from Sara.

"I tell people Tom was my only son, but he isn't. Wasn't. Daniel and I had another boy. He never made it into this world. I had a terrible drinking problem when Daniel and I were first married. I thought being married to someone as wonderful as Daniel would take all my problems away, but it never happens that way, does it? I lost the baby."

There was so much grief and regret in how Sara spoke the words. "I'm so sorry."

"So am I."

She shifted her weight, and Bridget wondered if she even realized how her hand strayed to her belly. To have lost not one child, but two—how did anyone keep on after something like that?

Bridget let Sara's words give her the courage to bring her secret out into the open. "Martina believes my father is her father." Sara was right—the words did loom large and dark in her head but seemed smaller and less powerful once spoken aloud.

"Oh, that is big."

"You're telling me. It changes everything."

"Do you believe she is your half sister?"

Bridget pulled her knees up and hugged them. "It explains a lot. My dad denies it."

Sara's eyes were kind. "The biggest secrets often get the loudest denials. So you didn't know until now. That's a long, old wound. Lots of pain. I get it."

"He's been lying to me," Bridget declared

almost too loudly. "Denying Martina. Maybe even lying to my mom. For years. And even faced with all this, with Martina and Matteo, he's still denying it. If Martina hadn't come here and did what she did, I don't think he'd ever have told me." She looked at Sara. "Who does that? Who walks around judging people like he does with this big fat lie sitting inside?" Shame at the sudden sharp outburst stung in her chest. "Sorry."

"Don't be," Sara replied. "That's just what secrets do. They cut us up on their way out into the world. Secret keeping is a sickening thing. It's often the ones carrying the biggest secrets that come down hardest on everyone around them. Like your father."

"Like my father," Bridget nearly muttered.

Sara waited a while before she spoke again. "You said it changes everything, but does it?"

"Of course, it does."

"Really?" Sara asked. "Does what he did change who you are? Does it change how you help the world?"

Bridget had to think about that. "I don't know."

"Well," Sara replied, "I think you get to decide that. If there's one thing life has taught me, it's that nobody gets to decide who you are but you."

Bridget shook her head. "I don't think it's that easy."

"Oh, I didn't say it was easy. Lots of times people and things try hard to tell you who you are. The question is, who are you going to listen to? That's faith—choosing which voice guides you."

That seemed like too simple a way to put it. Still, it did explain the steadfast spirit Bridget so admired in the woman. Dad was telling her she was naïve and being used. Could she really choose not to listen to that voice? Did the pain it caused really drown out the earlier voice that was telling her how much good she was doing here?

Bridget looked into Sara's eyes and saw so much compassion there. "How did you choose? How did you shut out the other stuff?"

Sara's sigh was deep with sadness. "I didn't always. And there were a few times I listened to the wrong people and gave the lies more power than they deserved." She looked down the hill to the memorial garden where Carson had resumed work on the wall, with Daniel and Leo helping him. Those three had become a team, making surprising progress on the project. "A lot of it came from Daniel. There were many times he saw things more clearly. I think that's the best part of having someone who loves you. They see what you're too tired or hurt or beaten to see." Sara smiled as the sound of a laugh from Leo came up the hill on a small and welcome breeze. "I know Daniel did that for me. Still does."

"I don't have that person. Not anymore. Maybe I only thought I had him in the first place."

"Oh, that's right." Sara gave Bridget's arm a soft, motherly pat. "You came here on the heels of a broken engagement. That's got to knock anyone off balance for a while." Her gaze traveled back down to where the three workers were busy lining up stones. "Only, are you so sure you don't have someone who sees the best parts of you?" She looked back at Bridget and raised one eyebrow in a silent question.

"I've felt a lot of support from Dana and Mason," Bridget replied, trying to avoid where she could see Sara was heading. "Even despite all the grief my dad's given them."

"I have no doubt that's true, but I was thinking more along personal lines." Sara smiled and nodded in Carson's direction.

The older woman definitely had a talent for

pulling truth out of people. "I think everybody has figured out that Carson and I have a…history." It struck Bridget at that moment that she couldn't clearly say whether she'd ended things with Carson that first time, or if Dad had convinced her and ended it for her. She found that lack of certainty disturbing.

"Having a history is one thing." Sara grunted as she pushed herself to her feet. "But if you ask me, the real question here is whether you have a future. Can you help each other see the strengths you each have? Or the ones you might have together." She pointed at Bridget. "*That's* the question worth asking."

In the space of one conversation, Sara had poked her way so far into Bridget's life—and with such undeniable wisdom and grace—that Bridget could only ask, "Are you always like this?"

Her reply was a playful wink. "Pretty much. Daniel tells me it's one of my better qualities." And with that, Sara made her way down the hill, waving a greeting to Carson, Daniel and Leo.

Bridget sat on the hill for a while longer, pondering all the wisdom Sara had given her. *I think that's the best part of having someone who loves you. They see what you're too tired or hurt or beaten to see.*

With a pang, she recalled what Carson had said to her last night. "I see how strong you are now. Let me help you see it."

Perhaps her future wasn't somewhere else. Perhaps God was trying to show her how it had been here all along.

Chapter Eighteen

The families gathered around the pond where a little table had been spread with a cheery cloth and a selection of flowers. Carson stood with the rest of the staff, keenly aware of the distance between him and Bridget. He yearned to stand near her as she watched this ritual. It would go straight to her compassionate heart. *Thank You for keeping her here long enough to see this*, he prayed. *She needs to see this.* Knowing it was pointless to think God didn't already see his heart, Carson added, *Please don't let her go. I'm begging You, don't make me watch her go.*

And then, as he thought of what Mason had said to him earlier this afternoon, Carson forced himself to amend his prayer. *Unless it's what You think she needs.*

It was always Charlie's job to explain the ceremony. He did a wonderful job, and it always amazed Carson how this family had created such a place of healing and comfort. He'd seen this event before, and each time it had helped to convince him this was a good place to make a true difference in the world.

"My mom was from Hawaii," Charlie began, "and this is how they remember the people who are gone. So we do it here. You can pick whatever flowers you want and say whatever you want. You don't even have to say anything at all, really. Just put your flower in the water and let it float out."

It sounded simple, but it never was. Many of the adults struggled through tears. Still, it seemed to reach the children most. When the breeze began to send the blooms out over the water, Dana always said there was grace in the wind. He didn't doubt it.

"I'll start," Charlie announced, as if it were the most natural thing in the world. Perhaps to him, it was. He'd been doing it his whole life, Mason said, as Charlie's mom, Melony, had passed down her island heritage to her son. The year Dana had arrived to pose the idea of launching Camp True North Springs, the pond had dried up. That's where the little fountain and ceramic frog Franco had come on the scene, serving as a stand-in pond until "God sent the weather—" as Mason put it "—to send us our pond back."

Carson swallowed the lump in his throat as Charlie picked four blooms and walked onto the dock. "We remember Tutu Kane. That's my grandpa." He placed a pale blue flower onto the water with an adorable solemnity. "And we remember Tutu Wahine. That's my grandma." A yellow flower went into the water, with Charlie tapping it gently so that it traveled toward the blue bloom. "They go together."

Carson ventured a glance at Bridget. Strong emotions played across her features. *How amazing it would be to be standing beside her the next time we do this.*

"We remember my other grandpa Dwight," Charlie said as he placed an orange flower onto the little ripples the breeze sent across the water. "And," Charlie went on, taking extra care with the final big pink flower, "we always remember Mama." The boy's voice was sad but strong.

Dana reached out her hand to Mason, and Carson marveled again at the amazing thing God had done in bringing Dana here. It was always good to know families healed from tragedy, but it was another thing altogether to watch it play out right in front of you in the lives of the Avery family. No matter what anyone said about his professional prospects—or lack of them—Carson was proud to be part of what the camp did.

"Anyone who wants to can go next," Charlie said. "There's more than enough for everybody."

After a small pause, little Missy Jennings tugged her father and two brothers toward the table of flowers. Carson's memory cast back to Missy's first day, when Bridget had so tenderly bandaged the little girl's sore finger. He realized, now, that he had begun to fall for Bridget all over again that day. Her kindness drew him, and her unnecessary doubts made him long to protect her.

It struck him, at that moment, that his urges to fix things for Bridget were pointless. What he truly needed was for Bridget to fix *him*. Or help him fix himself, to have the courage to step into the potential people kept telling him he had. He was the one with pointless doubts, not her. And while she hadn't given him much hope of any future together, Carson still knew in his bones that Bridget was the path to the man he could be. She was the woman who would lead him to the best parts of himself.

The brothers held their little sister tightly as Missy bent over to send a big white flower off the dock into the water. "We remember Mom," Rob said, bravely battling the crack in his voice. Carson wondered how these children would ever find the grace to forgive the man who'd opened fire in the grocery store and stolen their mother from them.

That shooter hadn't just stolen a mother; he'd stolen a wife, as well. Carson doubted any eye in the county was dry as Doug silently walked to the water and released a red flower. The widower said no words, only choked back the sob everyone seemed to be feeling. Carson glanced over to see Bridget wiping her eyes. It was beyond sad, but also healing. Somehow part of the sorrow floated away as the flowers made their way out into the pond.

One by one, each of the families chose blooms, declared their remembrances and sent the flowers out onto the water. Dana was right—there was something poignant in how the flowers found each other. "I always imagine all those lost loved ones saying hello," she said after the last ceremony Carson had witnessed. "Gathering together to send down grace onto all of us left behind."

Carson watched Bridget as Matteo and Martina finally stepped up to select flowers. Martina looked uncertain, as if her deception to Bridget had forfeited her right to take part in the ceremony. Earlier this afternoon, Carson had overheard Sara Lohan fiercely defending and encouraging Martina.

"You did what mothers do," Sara had said. "You did whatever it took to get your baby what you thought he needed. What he still might need. You've got some apologizing to do, but don't you write all this off as beyond redemption. God's bigger than that. It might take a while, but grace is a stubborn, persistent thing."

Carson had made his mind up as he'd walked away from that overheard conversation that he would be just that: a man of stubborn, persistent grace. *I won't give up on Bridget even if she drives out of this gate tonight*, he declared to God. *And I'll count on You to do the same.*

Mom had always used the term "a heart full to bursting" as a happy thing. As she watched the ceremony of floating flowers, though, Bridget found her heart full to bursting with sorrow, sadness, compassion, grace and a hundred other enormous feelings.

I've lost a loved one, too. It seemed selfish to think that way, but today her relationship with her parents felt damaged. She could only hope not beyond repair. *I feel like I can't trust anything.*

She tried to draw perspective from the grief and grace playing out in front of her. They were seeking healing despite lives that had changed forever.

Some losses really are forever—well, this side of Heaven, anyway, she told herself. *I haven't lost Dad. I've just lost my trust in him. I know I should lay that at Your feet, but I can't yet. Help me find my way out of this, or at least toward what to do next.*

She watched Sara Lohan clutch the dark red flower she'd chosen. Pain seemed to press down on her, and she struggled to release Tommy's flower out across the water. Letting go seemed to ask so much strength of a soul. Strength Bridget didn't have yet.

Still, her time here had taught her how strength came from being together. Dana had told her to watch how the flowers—for reasons no one could ever really explain—seemed to gather together as they floated out on the pond.

They circled around each other the same way the families gathered during their stay here. It wasn't running away—even to someplace as alluring as the *Brilliance* and the whole wide world—that would solve her problems. They merely followed her. It was the connections to people who loved you—truly loved you—that made healing possible. Had she found that here? In the camp, and perhaps even in Carson?

She was so lost in her thoughts that she hadn't even realized most of the families had headed back toward the treats set out on the big house porch. She looked down to find Charlie staring up at her, with Carson lingering a careful distance away.

"There's flowers left, Nurse Bridget. Do you want any? Dad says you've been sad. Is someone gone from you?"

Bridget swallowed hard at the boy's sweet generosity. *Gone.* There were some things in her life that felt gone this day, all right. Not in the same way as the other families, but Charlie was right—grief was grief.

"In a way," she managed to say despite the tightening in her throat, which threatened the arrival of tears.

"Well, that's what the flowers are for. It's

kinda hard—I get it—but kinda good, too. I always feel better after I do it, and I've done it lots of times." Charlie shrugged. "See you back up at the big house."

Bridget watched him leave, keenly aware that it left her alone with the flowers and with Carson. She was grateful not to be alone. So much so that the urge to fall into his arms and weep rose up hard enough to make her dizzy. She sank down on the little bench and sent him a pleading look.

He walked over and sat near but not too near. "I think you should," he said softly. "It's not the same kind of loss, but you have to let go of it all the same."

He understood. Of course, he understood. She wiped her eyes. "I'm overreacting."

"No, you're not. You've had the rug pulled out from underneath you while you were already off balance. Hard to take a double whammy like that."

She watched the flowers milling peacefully toward the center of the pond. It was beautiful. It should be soothing, but she felt like too much of a tangle to be anything close to soothed.

"How do I fix this? I mean there's no changing what I know, what is. Nothing's really changed but everything's changed. Where do I go from here?"

Carson spread his palms over his knees the way he did when he was struggling to say something. She knew that about him. She knew a lot of things about him, including the fact that he would never lie to her.

"How you heal from this is up to you," he said. "Who you become out from under Arthur's expectations? That's all up to you." He turned toward her, eyes as warm as she'd ever seen them. "But I want to be there to see it. I want, like you wouldn't believe, for where you go from here to be right here." He shook his head. "I'm not sure that made any sense."

It made more sense than just about anything else. Only the uncertainty and doubt were shouting so loud over his quiet declaration.

"You have to know I love you. I've never stopped, and I don't think I ever will. I've made some mistakes trying to help, but…" He grasped her hand. "Please, please let me help you. Stay. Here. We'll figure it out together. You belong here. I can see it so clearly even if you can't yet. God brought you here, back to me. I know your dad and Martina mucked it up a bit, but you *are here*." Carson reached up and touched the hair blown across her cheek by the small breeze. "Part of you wants to stay, I can see it. I think everyone can see it. Can you, even just a bit?"

So much of her wanted to stay. She just didn't think she could. Still, he could see enough strength in her. And he had strength, such strength. If no one else could see it, she could. This place had taught her what was truly important. *Who* was truly important. She allowed herself to feel the warm solid sensation that came when she tilted her face to lean into the palm of his hand. "Maybe just a bit."

The slow smile that crept across his face was full of love. Full of a solidness she knew she could trust. "A bit is all I need, B." He leaned slightly toward her, testing whether she'd pull away. She didn't. And while leaning closer to him was the smallest gesture, it felt as large as the mountains.

"I want us to be what we were to each other. Only better. I know you feel it. We can be *so much better* together." His face was so near she could feel the warmth coming off him; she felt herself falling into the sparkle of his eyes. "Will you let us?"

She answered his question with a kiss. Light, cautious and tender, but oh so perfect. Familiar and new at the same time. The breezy touch became full of power and healing as Carson wrapped his arms around her and returned the kiss. Deep, full of love and the power to bring her unstable world back to some form of balance. What better balance to a painful truth than this joyful truth? Feeling the joy radiate off him—off both of them—it was easy to believe God had sent her here. Martina's suggestion had been for questionable reasons, but look what God had done with it. What He could still be doing with it. Couldn't she trust that in the face of dealing with Dad? Couldn't she dare to believe Carson was part of who she could be?

Carson kissed the stream of tears that had wet her cheeks. "Do you know what it took for me not to charge up that hillside and beg you not to leave? Mason had to practically nail me to the dock."

Bridget found a small, surprising laugh come up from the tightness that had bound her chest for what felt like days. "Wait…didn't you already beg me not to leave last night?"

His smile was wide and brilliant. "Maybe just a bit."

"Turns out a bit was all I needed," she admitted. None of the situation had changed, but the struggle of it had lifted. Not all the way, but enough.

Bridget let her head fall against the strength of his shoulder, a deep exhale leaving her with a little more peace. The first day they'd sat here, the day she'd drawn a firm line between their hearts, now felt a million miles away. With Carson beside her, she found she could trust God could make His harmony from the clashing pieces of her current life.

Without a word, Bridget stood and selected a dark blue flower from those that still lay on the table. She didn't know where her relationship with Dad went from here, but God did. God had known all of the twists and turns this month had taken, and He knew the path to healing no matter how long it might take. Or even if it didn't come at all. Whatever the outcome, the next step was to release it into His hands.

Carson stood back as she walked to the edge of the dock, ready to let her take this step on her own. Instead, she held out her hand in invitation. She didn't need to do this alone.

He held her hand as she tossed the blue flower into the water. It bobbed and tumbled at first, but then righted itself to float away.

"I'm going to take that as a sign," Carson

said. "Things will tumble for a bit but eventually right themselves out."

"Maybe."

"Um…maybe sooner than you think," he said, pointing to the camp's front gate as it slid open.

Mom's car was coming down the driveway.

Chapter Nineteen

Bridget had never expected to see her mother's car coming through the gate.

Carson squinted into the sunset. "Isn't that your mom?"

"It is."

"Did you ask her to come see you?"

"I haven't talked to either of them since…" Bridget swallowed. She saw only one figure in the car. "And she's come on her own." Bridget's wounded heart stung a bit more at the fact. She hadn't realized she'd been holding on to hope that Dad would reach out, would recognize her pain. Still, Mom was here. That had to be worth something.

"I should go," Carson said. "You two need to talk."

Bridget took his hand. "No. Stay. I'm done

trying to untangle this all by myself. Please stay." She looked up at him, glad to feel the strength his gaze seemed to give her. "I want you to stay."

Carson wrapped his hand around hers. "You got it."

Bridget looked back to the porch of the big house, where Dana stood. She had to have been the one to let Mom through the gate. Dana somehow waved a *You okay?* question, and Bridget waved an assurance back. She could see the moment where Dana caught sight of her hand joined with Carson's, a smile crossing the woman's face. Had everyone been waiting for her to reconcile with Carson? Not including Mom and Dad, surely. Funny how that didn't matter so much anymore.

Her mother got out of the car as if she had ventured onto thin ice. In many ways, hadn't she? As she walked toward them, Mom noticed Bridget's hand clasped within Carson's. Her eyebrows arched more in surprise than Dana's approval.

Yes, Bridget declared silently, *we're together again*.

Bridget opted to take control of the situation. "Hello, Mom. I'm surprised to see you."

Mom clutched her handbag. "Can we talk?"

Bridget motioned toward the pair of benches. How perfect that Mason had brought a second one out for the ceremony. The coincidence bolstered Bridget's confidence that this conversation was no surprise to God.

Mom's glance darted back and forth between Bridget and Carson. "Alone?"

"Carson already knows all of it. I'd like him to stay."

Her mother's back straightened just a bit as she took a prim seat on the other bench. "Carson does not know all of it. Nor do you."

If she'd wanted the whole truth, maybe now she would get it. "I'm upset and hurt, but I'll try to listen." Then she thought to add, "Does Dad know you're here?" The answer would be telling.

"No." Mom's tone spoke much more than the simple word.

She set her handbag on the seat and then folded her hands. She was working up to something, so Bridget let her take the time she seemed to need.

"Your father," Mom began, looking down at her hands, "*is* Martina's father." Discomfort at the declaration curled her fingers into tight fists. Martina had insisted it was true, but her mother's statement somehow planted the fact solidly into the world. Carson's hand tightened around Bridget's, a silent show of support.

It was true. Bridget had felt its truth from the moment Carson told her, and more so when Martina had said it, but now she truly *knew* it. She waited for the world to feel shifted—to reel as it had back at the highway gas station when Carson first had the courage to tell her. It didn't happen.

There was really only one question to ask now. "Did you know?"

Mom sat up straight and looked Bridget in the eye. "Yes."

That didn't feel like enough of an explanation. "For how long?"

"Your father and I went through a rough patch just before you were born. I had a difficult pregnancy, and he doesn't deal with such things well."

That was true. Dad had precious little patience for weakness, illness or anything that didn't go the way he planned. Mom had always been the tender caretaker. It wasn't until her relationship with Carson—the first time—that Bridget realized tenderness was a personality trait, not a gender trait. It had stunned her that men could be gentle and caring, and it was why she'd fallen so deeply for Carson and later for

Anders's compassionate character. Now she knew tenderness and compassion could also be fierce and strong. Those were not the same thing as status—they were far more valuable.

"Two weeks after you were born, I found a note from Gabriella Perez, Martina's mother, in your father's jacket pocket. She was a secretary at the town hall. He was on the zoning board even then, so Arthur spent a lot of time there." Mom paused briefly, and Bridget could see the pain of this admission. "It was a brief thing, but that's not really the point of all this, is it? I was devastated, of course. Humiliated. Angry and feeling helpless with this tiny new baby—you—in my arms."

Mom didn't seem to be done, so Bridget kept silent. She couldn't think of what to say in any case.

"Your father did what your father does well—he solved it. He told me no one would ever know, that in exchange for Gabriella's silence he would send support. She was married, so it was all rather possible if everyone kept the secret. He tried—several times—to get the Perez family to move out of town, but they never did."

"But they're in Scottsdale now." Had Dad finally worn them down?

"I found it ironic that they moved there after Martina married and went to Milwaukee. But while they were here, Martina looked so much like her mother that there was never any question. After a while, I suppose we all rather convinced ourselves it had never even happened at all."

"Was he sorry?" Bridget was surprised at the sharp tone of her own words.

Mom's lips tightened. "Your father isn't a man of regrets. He doesn't admit to being wrong. I won't say it was easy, but we got past it."

Got past it? This was Martina they were talking about, not some misguided town ordinance or a regrettable purchase. "And you could live with that? Both of you?"

Mom's eyes grew defensive. "Times were different then. All families have secrets. I'm not saying I'm proud of how we handled it, but there were never serious consequences. We hoped you would never know."

The hurt rose up past Bridget's level of control. "Do you know what it felt like to find this out from Carson? Who heard it from Martina? When I should have heard it from Dad or at least you ages ago?" A panic crept up her spine. "What else don't I know? Is Dad my father?

Was the money you gave me to get on board the *Brilliance* really a gift or were you buying my way out of town to get me away from Carson?"

"Bridget…" Carson put a hand on her shoulder and tried to catch her eyes. "Take it easy."

"No. I won't take it easy." Bridget shot off the bench and paced the small stretch of land in front of the dock. "I'm upset. No, I'm undone. You lied to me. And now a little boy's life is at stake because no one could own up to the truth, so I *will not* take it easy."

"That little boy's life is not at stake—" Mom started.

"It could be," Bridget shot back. "We don't know he won't need bone marrow. I get that it's a long shot that I could be his donor, but Dad was ready to make sure no one from here had that chance. All to keep quiet what we found out, anyway. Does no one else here see how messed up that is?"

"Your mom is here," Carson said entirely too calmly. "She's trying to talk to you. Give her credit for that."

Bridget looked back to see tears in her mother's eyes. "I'm sorry," she said. "I'm sorry for all of it. We should have told you. When you were old enough to understand, we should have told you."

It was the one thing Bridget most wanted to hear. *I'm sorry.* She looked up at the sky, feeling small and raw. There was so much to regret in how this had all unfolded. No one had prevented any pain, really. They'd just delayed it.

Carson caught Bridget's gaze and nodded toward Mom, a silent *go over to her* in his eyes. She was angry with her mother, but Bridget lay the real blame at her father's feet. And Carson was right, she *was* here. Trying to do something about all this, even though no one seemed to know what ought to be done. At a loss for words, Bridget simply walked over and slipped her hand into her mom's. A small sob came from her mother as a result.

"I'm proud of you," Mom said in a quiet, wobbly voice. "I should say that more, but I don't. I just let life happen to me, but you, you're making choices even when they're hard. Fighting for what you think is best for you. I'm proud of that. I hope you can accept that someday if you can't right now."

"What I want, is to be with Carson. And to be here, at this camp." Bridget was amazed how easily the words came, how they sat in her soul without any resistance. "But I don't know how I can do that with Dad being the way he is."

"That's really what you want?"

"I'm sure of it."

Mom paused for a long moment, then pulled in a deep breath. "Then I won't get in your way. And as for your father, you leave him to me. Maybe it's time for me to learn how much of a fighter I can be, too."

Carson kept his arm around Bridget as they watched her mother drive past the gate.

"I love you." He'd said it half a dozen times in the last fifteen minutes and intended to keep it up for as long as he could.

"I love you, too. Thank you for helping me with her," Bridget said. "Turns out I don't have to go, or do this on my own."

He pulled her close. "Don't you dare leave me now. I've waited too long for this. You won't have to do any of this alone. Not your dad, not this camp, not the donor drive, none of it. At this rate, I may not even let you cross the street alone."

She slanted him a look. "Don't you get controlling on me. I've had a lifetime of that."

Point taken. "How about a lifetime of a guy being madly in love with you?"

She kissed him. Bridget wrapped her arms around his neck, and he felt as if he'd pulled all the happiness in the world down into this little moment. "I like that idea." He loved all the joy and relief he could hear in her voice. "But we've got a donor drive to run and a camp session to wrap up. I'd settle for you helping me get through the next few days."

Carson held her tight, marveling in how she felt so perfect in his arms. Just like before, only so much better. "You got it. The 'madly in love' part comes with the deal."

Her head fell against his chest, all the tension of the day dissolving under the indigo sky just starting to set out its array of stars. "My dad was so wrong about you."

"Not entirely," he admitted.

That pulled her head up in surprise. "Oh, he was terrible about it, but there was an irritating bit of truth in what he said. I've ignored opportunities. Refused good prospects just to play the rebel who didn't care. But I could be more. I should be more. No more ditching self-respect. I want to know I have your respect."

"You do," Bridget insisted. "I know I didn't see it before, but you need to know I do now." She put her hand on his heart and he felt the warmth of it in every corner of his soul. "You are good and kind and strong in all the ways that matter. I'm sorry if I ever let you believe that wasn't true."

He kissed the top of her head, delighting in the sheer bliss of it. "Thank you. But you should know I'm going to talk to Gordon about that apprenticeship. I think I'd make a top-notch electrician."

Bridget's eyes shone bright. "I know I feel the spark."

"You save up jokes like that?" He smiled as he pulled her close. "Honestly, tonight I feel as if there's nothing you and I can't tackle." They still had a bunch of hurdles to jump, but he had Bridget, and that meant absolutely anything was possible.

"Speaking of possibilities, I hear there's a permanent nursing position open at this camp. I'm still only the temporary nurse, you know."

He grinned. "I happen to know the owners. Rumor has it they're rather fond of you. You're so invested in this place, it's seeping out of your pores. Trust me, it's all done but the paperwork. Camp True North Springs has its forever nurse." *And I have my forever love*, his heart whispered.

"I want to stay. Here. With you." She nestled against him, and her softening was the most spectacular sensation he could imagine. After a moment, she tilted her head up to face him. "Do you think this is what God had planned all along? In all the twists and turns and things we never saw coming?"

"Yeah, I do." He had no doubt. Turns out Camp True North Springs heals more than just the families who come to visit. Maybe he could trust that God would find a way to heal the rift between Bridget and her father. It seemed a near impossibility, but Mason was always saying God delighted in long shots. "I think it's all going to turn out okay."

"You know, this is the first time in a while I actually think that's true." After a moment, she asked, "Is it always like this?"

Carson laughed. "We get our share of drama. And happiness, too. Seb and Kate, Mason and Dana—" he looked down at her "—and now Carson and Bridget. We keep this up and Camp True North Springs could get a reputation for finding love as much as the hope and healing stuff."

She giggled, a delightful, joyful noise that went straight to his heart. "That's a stretch."

"Oh, I don't know. I mean, this session's over at the end of this week. There's another one behind it. Who knows what that will bring?" He kissed her again, just for the sheer delight of doing so. "I'm just glad you'll be here with me for all of it.

"Have I mentioned that I love you?" he whispered into her ear.

"Repeatedly," she murmured back.

"Well, given that I botched it the first time, I've got some making up to do."

She laughed. "I still can't believe you told my father before you told me." She pushed up off him for a moment, pointing out over the pond. "Look."

The flowers had drifted to the far side of the pond, still in the little floating island grouping they'd managed to make. The dark blue flower Bridget had sent out in her father's name, however, had never joined that collection. It had spent the entire time bobbing on its own. Carson had noticed this and wondered if Bridget had seen the poignant image.

"Look at him. He's all alone," she said. Her words had a mixture of bitterness and sorrow.

The bloom was close to the dock, meandering the shoreline in sad circles. "Maybe not," Carson ventured, surprised he could muster up a shred of sympathy for the man. "Maybe he's just trying to come back and doesn't know how."

Chapter Twenty

The town square in North Springs was bustling with people and activity. Busketeers offered up pancakes while a team of volunteers signed up bone marrow donors. A squad of staff from LifeGift was busy distributing forms and doing the necessary swab tests. Bridget took in the whole scene, heart full to bursting—in a good way. *I'm so grateful I didn't miss this*.

"We just topped two hundred," Carson announced, his smile matching the one Bridget knew spread across her own face. She hadn't stopped smiling all morning. "And it doesn't look like we're even close to done."

Rita Salinas nodded as she walked by with more supplies for the Busketeers. "This is the North Springs I know. Big hearts. And big stomachs." After lining up for their own donor registries, the Busketeers hadn't stopped cooking for everyone who participated.

Bridget felt as if she were finally revisiting the town of her happy childhood memories. Maybe the darker challenges of the past few years would be balanced out by the prospect of a happy future. She squeezed Carson's hand. "Thank you for keeping me here."

He kissed her. "Thanks for staying. You should be here to see this. You should be here, period. And I'm glad you are."

"Me, too." She looked around again. "Have you seen Martina and Matteo?"

"Dana told me they were coming a bit later. She didn't want him to get overwhelmed with all the attention, and they're going to meet with Fiona when she gets here."

Martina was a good mother. Bridget could see that. It had just come out in the wrong ways. Fear and secrets could bring out the worst impulses in people, but perhaps that made it a place where grace and forgiveness could be so powerful.

A short while later, Fiona came walking across the square. She spread her arms to the bustle of activity and grinned. "These are always the best parts of my job. You've put together an amazing drive. We're grateful, really."

Fiona didn't know of the family tensions involved in this particular drive. Bridget chose simply to smile at the show of thanks. "It was way easier than I thought once people realized there weren't any needles involved."

Fiona gestured toward a bench in one corner of the square. "Can we sit down?"

The three of them walked over and took a seat under the shade of a tree. Fiona pulled out a file. "This may go down as one of my favorite stories for a long time."

"I really am glad we were able to help," Bridget said.

"It's more than that," Fiona said. The woman took a deep breath. "Bridget, you're a match. For Matteo."

The words hit Bridget like a burst of sunshine. "I... I am?"

"I can't even begin to tell you the odds against it, but, yes, you're a match. You can donate bone marrow for Matteo to have a transplant. You can give him a strong shot at a long and healthy future."

"I'm a match." Bridget tried to absorb the enormity of what she'd just heard.

"The odds are astronomical. It's astounding. The statistics against it…"

"God doesn't seem to care much about stats," Carson said. "He had this whole thing set up from the beginning, if you ask me."

"I think maybe you're right," Fiona said. "I haven't got another explanation." She looked at Bridget, who was wiping away tears. "Are you okay?"

"I'm wonderful," Bridget said with a sniffle. "Stunned, but wonderful. Have you told Martina? She said she was going to meet up with you in a bit."

"I thought maybe we'd tell her together. Is that okay? Like I said, this is one of the most remarkable stories I've seen in a long time."

"Martina said she believed there was a match here in North Springs." The truth was much more complicated than that, but Bridget felt she could share that much.

"I'm glad she was right. And who knows how many other matches are here among the tests. I always feel such hope when we do one of these. There are a lot of noes in my work, but the yeses always make up for them ten times over."

It was true. This yes did make up ten times over for the pain it had taken to get here. That didn't take all the problems away, but it did give her a full supply of courage to take them on. Especially with Carson beside her. She swept her gaze across the crowd of people with a prayer of thanksgiving in her heart.

A heart that stopped when she saw two people walking onto the square. Mom and Dad. They were here. Talk about your astronomical odds—she'd never expected them to show at this event.

"Would you excuse me?" she said to Fiona. "I need to go talk to someone."

"Who?" Carson asked, until he followed Bridget's gaze. "You ready to do that?"

She was. "I'm okay. I'll catch up with you in a bit. Go help Fiona get some of those pancakes, and I'll be back."

Carson gave her an "Are you sure?" look until she nodded and rose off the bench. It was time to make use of that courage.

Mom and Dad looked uncomfortable but determined—Mom especially. "Hi," Bridget said, pleased at the steadiness of her voice despite how her emotions seemed to be launching fireworks in her chest. "I'm glad to see you."

"A lot of people showed up."

Bridget wasn't sure if her mother meant it as a compliment or a simple statement of fact.

"Over two hundred sign-ups so far. Fiona from LifeGift says she's thrilled."

Dad said nothing, but scanned his eyes over the event.

Bridget took a deep breath. "I'm a match, Dad. I can donate for Matteo's transplant."

Mom and Dad looked stunned. "You said the odds were totally against you matching," Mom said.

She smiled. "I think Carson put it best when he said God doesn't seem to care about statistics. It's nothing short of a wonder. I'm hoping you can see that."

Dad looked at her, his gaze a collection of so many emotions. In some way it felt as if he'd truly seen her for the first time. The coldness that so often sat in his eyes was indeed giving way to the wonder that was filling her heart. Making her believe that God had other wonders ready to show her.

"Maybe," he said simply. For him, though, the single word was a huge response.

The urge to hug him rose up with astonishing clarity. She did, and when he softened against her and whispered, "Bridget," all the bitterness between them started to dissolve. It wasn't the solution of everything, but it was a start.

"They're here," Mom said softly, concern putting an edge on her words. "Maybe we should go."

Bridget looked over to see Martina and Matteo making their way onto the square.

"Don't go," she pleaded. "Stay. I know it's hard, but please stay."

Dad stilled for a second, the years of secrecy and denial forcing his back straight and his jaw tight. She waited for him to turn and leave. To her surprise, he didn't. Out of the corner of her eye, she caught sight of Carson, who'd seen what she'd seen. She heard his voice in her heart. *God had this whole thing set up from the beginning, if you ask me.*

Bridget slipped her hand into her father's. "Come with me, Dad. I want to introduce you to someone."

Come to the garden after supper, the note said.

The families had all gone home, and the camp was quiet and empty. Bridget was worried it would feel lonely with only the staff here, but instead it felt at peace. Spacious. Resting and restoring for the next weary souls Camp True North Springs would welcome.

As she made her way up the small hillside, the dark of the memorial garden suddenly lit up with a brilliant collection of tiny lights strung along the wall and the archway. It looked like a carnival, or Christmas in the middle of the summer. She hadn't remembered them talking about lighting the garden at the final staff meeting, and besides, there were no guests here now.

Ah, but she wasn't alone.

There, in the corner of the glow cast by the galaxy of lights, stood Carson. He made a dramatic show of holding the connected plugs, the delighted master of this twinkling creation. "Like it?" he said with a grin.

"It's beautiful. The families will love it."

Carson set the wiring down and walked toward her. "It's not for the families. This is for you. Consider it my first electrical feat."

She felt a smile spread across her face. "You were accepted into the apprenticeship?" The move had been a big leap for him, and she was so pleased to see it had gone well.

"Never a moment's doubt, according to Gordon. I'll be a licensed electrician by—" he made a show of checking his watch "—nine hundred hours of classroom time and about eight thousand hours of on-the-job training. So I should be done by the fall."

Bridget laughed. "You mean you'll be done in…how many years?"

He shrugged. "Four to five. Plenty of time to devote to Camp True North Springs. And with some of the wiring in this place, it might take that long." He took her hands in his. "How do you feel about long engagements?"

Bridget's breath caught. "What?"

"I know it's a bit early to talk like that, but not really when you think about it. We've clocked in a bunch of years already. But I want us to take our time and get it right. Perfect. I don't want to spend another day without knowing our futures will be together." He pulled her into a breathtaking kiss, one that made her insides glow brighter than ten times the wattage of the lights surrounding them.

When they were both able to catch their breath again, he grinned and said, "How long do you think it'll take?"

She could only laugh. "Not four years, that's for sure." Honestly, if he suggested running off into the night and eloping right now, Bridget couldn't truly say she'd decline. But there was no need to hurry. He was right—it would be a good thing to take time and get it absolutely perfect.

Carson stared into her eyes. "Marry me someday?"

She lost herself in the glow of his affection. "Yes. Someday soon."

Together they looked up at the stars strung across the heavens as if to celebrate the moment. "Soon sounds perfect."

* * * * *

Dear Reader,

How often we believe our past holds us back from the future God has waiting for us! If we could only trust in His ability to use all things for good, and in the power of grace and mercy, the world might be a very different place.

I hope you've enjoyed another visit to Camp True North Springs and the grace and mercy found there. If you've not discovered the previous books in the series, I invite you to read *A Place to Heal* and *Restoring Their Family*. You'll have a chance to come up the mountain another time later this year, as well.

My thanks to Marti Freund for helping me to get all the details of bone marrow donation accurate. If you would like more information about joining me on the bone marrow donor registry, please contact Gift of Life (giftoflife. org) or any local cancer support agency. Nothing would make me happier than knowing this story led someone to make this lifesaving gift.

As always, I love to hear from readers. You can find me on Instagram @alliepleiterauthor,

Facebook AlliePleiter, my website alliepleiter. com or via email at allie@alliepleiter.com.

Blessings to you—and thank you so much for reading!

Allie Pleiter

Get 3 FREE REWARDS!

We'll send you 2 FREE Books plus a FREE Mystery Gift.

FREE Value Over **$20**

Both the **Love Inspired**® and **Love Inspired**® Suspense series feature compelling novels filled with inspirational romance, faith, forgiveness and hope.

YES! Please send me 2 FREE novels from the Love Inspired or Love Inspired Suspense series and my FREE gift (gift is worth about $10 retail). After receiving them, if I don't wish to receive any more books, I can return the shipping statement marked "cancel." If I don't cancel, I will receive 6 brand-new Love Inspired Larger-Print books or Love Inspired Suspense Larger-Print books every month and be billed just $6.49 each in the U.S. or $6.74 each in Canada. That is a savings of at least 16% off the cover price. It's quite a bargain! Shipping and handling is just 50¢ per book in the U.S. and $1.25 per book in Canada.* I understand that accepting the 2 free books and gift places me under no obligation to buy anything. I can always return a shipment and cancel at any time by calling the number below. The free books and gift are mine to keep no matter what I decide.

Choose one: ☐ **Love Inspired Larger-Print**
(122/322 BPA GRPA)

☐ **Love Inspired Suspense Larger-Print**
(107/307 BPA GRPA)

☐ **Or Try Both!**
(122/322 & 107/307 BPA GRRP)

Name (please print)

Address   Apt. #

City   State/Province   Zip/Postal Code

Email: Please check this box ☐ if you would like to receive newsletters and promotional emails from Harlequin Enterprises ULC and its affiliates. You can unsubscribe anytime.

Mail to the **Harlequin Reader Service:**
IN U.S.A.: P.O. Box 1341, Buffalo, NY 14240-8531
IN CANADA: P.O. Box 603, Fort Erie, Ontario L2A 5X3

Want to try 2 free books from another series? Call 1-800-873-8635 or visit www.ReaderService.com.

*Terms and prices subject to change without notice. Prices do not include sales taxes, which will be charged (if applicable) based on your state or country of residence. Canadian residents will be charged applicable taxes. Offer not valid in Quebec. This offer is limited to one order per household. Books received may not be as shown. Not valid for current subscribers to the Love Inspired or Love Inspired Suspense series. All orders subject to approval. Credit or debit balances in a customer's account(s) may be offset by any other outstanding balance owed by or to the customer. Please allow 4 to 6 weeks for delivery. Offer available while quantities last.

Your Privacy—Your information is being collected by Harlequin Enterprises ULC, operating as Harlequin Reader Service. For a complete summary of the information we collect, how we use this information and to whom it is disclosed, please visit our privacy notice located at corporate.harlequin.com/privacy-notice. From time to time we may also exchange your personal information with reputable third parties. If you wish to opt out of this sharing of your personal information, please visit readerservice.com/consumerschoice or call 1-800-873-8635. **Notice to California Residents**—Under California law, you have specific rights to control and access your data. For more information on these rights and how to exercise them, visit corporate.harlequin.com/california-privacy.

LIRLIS23

Get 3 FREE REWARDS!

We'll send you 2 FREE Books plus a FREE Mystery Gift.

FREE Value Over **$20**

Both the **Harlequin® Special Edition** and **Harlequin® Heartwarming™** series feature compelling novels filled with stories of love and strength where the bonds of friendship, family and community unite.

YES! Please send me 2 FREE novels from the Harlequin Special Edition or Harlequin Heartwarming series and my FREE Gift (gift is worth about $10 retail). After receiving them, if I don't wish to receive any more books, I can return the shipping statement marked "cancel." If I don't cancel, I will receive 6 brand-new Harlequin Special Edition books every month and be billed just $5.49 each in the U.S. or $6.24 each in Canada, a savings of at least 12% off the cover price, or 4 brand-new Harlequin Heartwarming Larger-Print books every month and be billed just $6.24 each in the U.S. or $6.74 each in Canada, a savings of at least 19% off the cover price. It's quite a bargain! Shipping and handling is just 50¢ per book in the U.S. and $1.25 per book in Canada.* I understand that accepting the 2 free books and gift places me under no obligation to buy anything. I can always return a shipment and cancel at any time by calling the number below. The free books and gift are mine to keep no matter what I decide.

Choose one: ☐ **Harlequin Special Edition** (235/335 BPA GRMK)   ☐ **Harlequin Heartwarming Larger-Print** (161/361 BPA GRMK)   ☐ **Or Try Both!** (235/335 & 161/361 BPA GRPZ)

Name (please print)

Address   Apt. #

City   State/Province   Zip/Postal Code

Email: Please check this box ☐ if you would like to receive newsletters and promotional emails from Harlequin Enterprises ULC and its affiliates. You can unsubscribe anytime.

> ### Mail to the **Harlequin Reader Service:**
> **IN U.S.A.:** P.O. Box 1341, Buffalo, NY 14240-8531
> **IN CANADA:** P.O. Box 603, Fort Erie, Ontario L2A 5X3

Want to try 2 free books from another series! Call 1-800-873-8635 or visit www.ReaderService.com.

*Terms and prices subject to change without notice. Prices do not include sales taxes, which will be charged (if applicable) based on your state or country of residence. Canadian residents will be charged applicable taxes. Offer not valid in Quebec. This offer is limited to one order per household. Books received may not be as shown. Not valid for current subscribers to the Harlequin Special Edition or Harlequin Heartwarming series. All orders subject to approval. Credit or debit balances in a customer's account(s) may be offset by any other outstanding balance owed by or to the customer. Please allow 4 to 6 weeks for delivery. Offer available while quantities last.

Your Privacy—Your information is being collected by Harlequin Enterprises ULC, operating as Harlequin Reader Service. For a complete summary of the information we collect, how we use this information and to whom it is disclosed, please visit our privacy notice located at corporate.harlequin.com/privacy-notice. From time to time we may also exchange your personal information with reputable third parties. If you wish to opt out of this sharing of your personal information, please visit readerservice.com/consumerchoice or call 1-800-873-8635. **Notice to California Residents**—Under California law, you have specific rights to control and access your data. For more information on these rights and how to exercise them, visit corporate.harlequin.com/california-privacy.

HSEHW23

THE AMISH MARRIAGE ARRANGEMENT
Amish Country Matches • by Patricia Johns

Sarai Peachy is convinced that her *grossmammi* and their next-door neighbor are the perfect match. But the older man's grandson isn't so sure. When a storm forces the two to work together on repairs, will spending time with Arden Stoltzfus prove to Sarai that the former heartbreaker is a changed man?

THE AMISH NANNY'S PROMISE
by Amy Grochowski

Since the loss of his wife, Nick Weaver has relied on nanny Fern Beiler to care for him and his *kinner*. But when the community pushes them into a marriage of convenience, the simple arrangement grows more complicated. Will these two friends find love for a lifetime?

HER ALASKAN COMPANION
K-9 Companions • by Heidi McCahan

Moving to Alaska is the fresh start that pregnant widow Lexi Thomas has been looking for. But taking care of a rambunctious dog wasn't part of the plan. When an unlikely friendship blooms between her and the dog's owner, Heath Donovan, can she take a chance and risk her heart again?

THE RELUCTANT RANCHER
Lone Star Heritage • by Jolene Navarro

World-weary FBI agent Enzo Flores returns home to help his pregnant sister. When she goes into premature labor, he needs help to care for his nephew and the ranch. Will childhood rival Resa Espinoza step in to help and forgive their troubled past?

FALLING FOR THE FAMILY NEXT DOOR
Sage Creek • by Jennifer Slattery

Needing a fresh start, Daria Ellis moves to Texas with her niece and nephew. But it's more challenging than she ever imagined, especially with handsome cowboy Tyler Reyes living next door. When they clash over property lines, will it ruin everything or prove to be a blessing in disguise?

A HAVEN FOR HIS TWINS
by April Arrington

Deciding to right the wrongs of the past, former bull rider Holt Williams returns home to reclaim his twin sons. But Jessie Alden, the woman who's raised them all these years, isn't keen on the idea. Can he be trusted, or will he hurt his sons—and her—all over again?

LOOK FOR THESE AND OTHER LOVE INSPIRED BOOKS WHEREVER BOOKS ARE SOLD, INCLUDING MOST BOOKSTORES, SUPERMARKETS, DISCOUNT STORES AND DRUGSTORES.

LICNM0623

HARLEQUIN
PLUS

Try the best multimedia subscription service for romance readers like you!

Read, Watch and Play.

Experience the easiest way to get the romance content you crave.

Start your **FREE TRIAL** at
<u>www.harlequinplus.com/freetrial</u>.

HARPLUS0123